THE REVEALING

THE REVEALING

C. J. PLOGGER

RESOURCE *Publications* · Eugene, Oregon

THE REVEALING

Resource Publications
An Imprint of Wipf and Stock Publishers
199 W. 8th Ave., Suite 3
Eugene, OR 97401

www.wipfandstock.com

PAPERBACK ISBN: 978-1-7252-9164-5
HARDCOVER ISBN: 978-1-7252-9165-2
EBOOK ISBN: 978-1-7252-9166-9

02/10/21

This book is dedicated to Reverend Don Stout II
with much love and respect.
Don lived his life knowing the Revealer and
now he is celebrating in Paradise with Him.

THANK YOU!

- ◆ Debbie Stout, a wonderful woman who loved Don in a selfless and powerful manner.
- ◆ The editors at We Edit Books, Fran Allred and Mickey Johnson. They always challenge me which makes our projects much better.

ONE

Violently he tugged at his mint green and pink tie, as it seemed to grow tighter around his neck. His knee struck the corner of his sturdy oak desk. "Is there anything else that can go wrong tonight?" he muttered. It was a rhetorical question, not directed at anyone, but simply thrown out as a release of exasperation.

Pastor Don Stout rubbed his knee and sat down heavily on his padded chair, his tie limp across his white dress shirt. The office was crowded with steely gray file cabinets and tall bookshelves where his eyes wearily catalogued the volumes he had collected over the years. In the corner of the 1970s wallpapered walls was an antiquated air conditioner with only two settings, medium and high. His framed diplomas, carefully hung nearby, seemed to proclaim their importance.

After four years of Bible college and four years of seminary, he was now forging ahead with his application to be accepted for a Doctor of Ministry degree, which he hoped would add some value to his unappreciated calling. Don was frustrated. He was an intelligent man in his late 20s who truly loved the Lord, but felt swallowed up in the overwhelming expectations and unfair demands of the pastorate.

"This is not what I expected," he blurted out as he pressed his head between his hands over a coffee-stained desk calendar covered with yellow Post-It Notes. In Bible college, he had excelled in his studies and in seminary, his professors often publicly remarked how God was going to use him in the ministry someday. But when was that someday going to be? When was he going to change the world and rattle the gates of hell so forcefully that the devil himself would run out with his hands raised high, loudly crying out, "I surrender!"

Don had caught himself at times daydreaming during classes about what his ministry would look like. He saw himself standing in front of huge gatherings of eager people, sharing the good news of the Gospel, elegantly poised before a sea of smiling faces ready to hear the Biblical challenges their pastor would authoritatively issue and prophetically proclaim. Don had believed his first church would be a large, vibrant one that routinely would be the focus of bold headlines in far-ranging newspapers because it was transforming the world. But that has not been the case.

For the past three years, Don had served as the pastor of a small, obscure congregation tucked away in the southern part of Indiana, in a little town called Huron. It was nestled in the midst of a forest of trees, which quietly stood as looming sentries. In Huron, there were no stop lights, but there were four stop signs, a post office and a convenience store, which was open on Mondays, Tuesdays, and maybe Thursdays. When Sally Montgomery came home from the hospital last month with her fourth child, the population grew to 73 residents.

The nearest town was Bedford, which was about 15 miles away following twisting, curvy State Route 50. The closest large town was Bloomington, home of Indiana University, where famous basketball coach Bobby Knight infamously attempted to motivate his players by throwing chairs onto the hardwood court. Even though Bedford was not a major city, compared to Don's tiny burg, it seemed a sprawling metropolis, with a hospital and nursing home he visited regularly.

Don drove the twisting, snaking road to Bedford several times a week. It was also the location of the nearest Walmart and where he would meet with ministers of the local ministerial assembly. Don usually appreciated their time together; it gave him an opportunity to express his disappointments and rare victories.

But tonight, the night of the weekly Wednesday Bible study, Don felt the weight of inadequacy dragging him toward despair. The midweek study usually had four to six participants, who solemnly shuffled in and scattered out among the nine scarlet-red pews in the tiny sanctuary. This was Don's first church after seminary, but he had always envisioned teaching and preaching in a larger setting.

Some of Don's friends had joined the staff of larger congregations as associate pastors standing in front of hundreds of people every Sunday morning and leading effective ministries. Other colleagues had been granted parishes where people enthusiastically gathered to learn about God and change the world. But Don didn't feel this way. Every Sunday afternoon, he walked past the glossy, varnished attendance board, and his heart sank when it read 39 people this week, 36 last week.

Discouraged, Don imagined that the Bible studies of his coworkers included deep theological topics such as the mystery of the incarnation and the application of the Old Testament minor prophets to today's society. Don wondered in frustration because the dialogue in his studies seemed to turn quickly to topics such as how high the corn grew last month because of the rain and why Alan Smith's convenience store was not open last Thursday.

That night, it all seemed to cave in on him. Nothing out of the ordinary had happened, just the usual routine of chasing conversational rabbits with Margaret Altman instead of answering the Bible questions he asked. He did hear from Tom Majors that he had misquoted a scripture verse last Sunday morning and was chastised again by Julie Johnson that he really should be using the King James Version of the Bible instead of the "heretical" New International Version. Something within Don's spirit was crushed beyond repair. An overwhelming despondency settled upon his heart, weighing heavier than it ever had before.

Don knew the statistics of pastoral burnout but thought he would be the exception. He knew that God is more interested in our obedience than our perceived concept of success by having more people in the pews and more money in the bank. But still, Don felt that there must be more. He pulled his head from his hands and audibly cried out, "Lord, am I a failure? Lord, is this what ministry is all about? Is this it?"

That initial release opened a floodgate of emotions as the volume of Don's voice rose. "And another thing, God: I should be pastoring a larger church. I'm wasting my time here. The people are more interested in themselves than learning about you. They are more concerned about what they are going to bring to the next potluck instead of digging deeper as disciples. And another thing: every time I turn around, I'm getting criticized."

Don felt a twinge of guilt as he verbalized thoughts he had buried deep in his heart the past couple years. He felt contrite as the shame of selfishness seeped into his soul. "Lord, I'm sorry. I know that you are in control. I just feel like a failure. I don't think I have accomplished anything and I thought things were supposed to be different."

Don regained his composure and continued in his lecturing prayer, "Lord, if only I knew what people were thinking, I could help them. If only people would be real, I could make a difference. I would love to know what is going on in the hearts of people." Then with a boldness that shocked himself, Don proclaimed: "Lord, let me know what is going on in the hearts of people." Resigning himself to write this off as an exercise of self-pity, Don then chuckled. "Look at me, trying to tell God what to do."

What happened next seemed to take hours, but was over in minutes. Don felt his heavy, oversized desk start to shake, but it wasn't moving. The first idea that raced through his mind was that he didn't know there were earthquakes in southern Indiana. He scanned the room, but it was still. Then it appeared as if the room began to fill with smoke, but it wasn't smoke.

The air pressure seemed to be different and fear swelled within him. "What is going on?" he yelped.

Don felt transported to another place, another time. He was still in his office, surrounded by his books, but this was not the same place. Something radical was taking place. Something supernatural was occurring. A heavy presence filled the office, so much so that Don's breathing became labored. Scenarios darted through his mind. Was he having a heart attack? Was the stress of ministry finally exacting its toll on his mental faculties?

Don was confused and afraid, but also, and without explanation, he knew that he would not be harmed. Don knew that something was happening, but he had no clue what it was. He was trying to take it all in, but simply found himself paralyzed. The room was the same, but it was not. The appearance of the room had not changed, but something had. Don later could only describe the atmosphere of the room as being filled with glory, not really understanding his own explanation.

With all these notions consecutively scurrying through Don's mind, he heard a voice issue a query to him. The voice was not audible. Or was it? The voice was one of authority, but calm, strong but gentle, confident but not arrogant. Don was so rattled by the voice that his heart almost stopped beating.

"Donald, did I call you to serve me?"

Every hair on Don's body stood on edge as every nerve in his body tingled. "Is that you, Lord?"

"Donald, did I call you to serve me?" The voice seemed to echo through every chamber of Don's heart, petrifying him while soothing him. Completely opposite sensations were taking place all at once, letting Don know that he was somehow in the presence of the living Lord.

"Yes, Lord, you called me," he stuttered, feebly.

"What did I call you to do, Donald?" The voice was becoming more familiar, but was one that Don had never heard before in this capacity.

Don crumbled to the floor in a huddled, quivering mass, terrified and unable to look up or around. "Lord, you called me to serve you."

"Yes, I did. But right now, it seems you are only interested in how you can be served."

Don's heart was pierced as conviction surged through his soul and he began to weep. "Lord, I'm sorry. I have been selfish."

In a loving parental tone, the Lord replied, "You are forgiven, my son." Graceful words flooded Don's heart with encouragement and an emotional warmth spread through his soul, satisfying Don with a peace he had never felt before.

Don believed he had a good relationship with the Lord; he regularly spent time in the Word, learning about God and applying the lessons to his life. He often prayed by himself and with others, and there had been a few times when he felt they had stepped closer to knowing the Lord. But this was different. The Lord was speaking directly to him about an issue of his heart and had forgiven him.

Moved by God's mercy, Don stopped trembling and an immeasurable sense of gratitude overtook him.

"Thank you, Lord. I don't deserve your forgiveness. Thank you!" The words, "thank you," just seemed to repeat over and over again in his heart.

"Stand up, Donald," the Lord commanded.

"Yes, Lord," Don blurted without hesitation, and quickly rose to his feet. But then Don's mind reeled with questions. Was he supposed to keep his head bowed, or his eyes closed, or extend his hands in an outward expression of worship?

The Lord seemed to be amused at Don's disorientation and spoke softly to him. "Donald, you can relax. You are thinking too much."

"But Lord," Don said, then started thinking about how many people have said, "But Lord" to God. "When you passed by Moses, he could not look at You or else he would have died."

Again, as if Don's comments were humorous to him, the Lord replied, "Donald, you are not seeing me. I simply wanted to talk to you."

Don felt relieved, but was still unsure where to look, so he bent his head slightly toward the carpeted floor while keeping his eyes positioned so he could look up. As Don viewed his office, he was surprised because its appearance hadn't changed in any form, but, now, he saw things more clearly. It was as if his vision had dramatically improved and he could see what was really important.

The survey of his surroundings was cut short when the Lord spoke again. "Donald, you asked if I would let you know what was in the hearts of people."

Don barely remembered his earlier rantings and, again, shame rose. "Lord, I'm sorry, I was just upset, I . . ."

Before he could continue, the Lord said, "No, Donald, I have decided that I am going to let you know what is in the hearts of others for the next week."

Don's head snapped toward the ceiling. "I don't know what you mean, Lord?"

"I have decided that you will know what is in the hearts of others until next Wednesday evening at this very time."

Don's confusion not only showed on his face, but caused an involuntary shrugging of his shoulders. "Lord, I don't know what you mean. How am I going to know what is in the hearts of others? Are you going to send me an email? Are you going to give me a manual? Are you going to speak to me?"

"I am going to send you the Revealer," the Lord spoke matter-of-factly.

As with Don's spiritual journey, one question led to another. "Lord, I really don't understand what is happening."

"The Revealer will explain everything to you, and you will understand."

"Lord, I don't get it," Don protested, but sensed something was changing. The feeling in the room was different, not bad but not the same. When the Lord was speaking to Don, he was consumed by His presence, but now he perceived something was altered. Don still had the peace he experienced when he heard the Lord's voice, but, in an odd way, he felt alone.

Don wondered if he were going crazy; he had heard of other ministers snapping and imagining they were one of the Twelve Disciples or that they could feed thousands of people with a few fish and loaves of bread. "What just happened?" he mused. "I thought I was hearing the voice of the Lord." With these quizzical thoughts flooding his mind, he was startled when there was a knock on the door to his office.

"Who is it? This is Pastor Don," he said haltingly. He replayed in his mind what had happened after Bible study because he distinctly remembered locking the doors of the church. He couldn't forget locking the door because Stan Tolemski had been standing just inside the glass-doored landing, expressing his deep discontent that Mike Byrd had said "Amen" in last week's service. Don recalled nodding his head in feigned agreement, quickly ushering Stan out the door and turning the latch as he said goodnight.

The door slowly opened and a man a couple of inches taller than Don, with a medium build, poked his head inside. The unplanned visitor smiled warmly and broke the ice, "Are you ready?"

Don had never seen the man before, but there was a strange familiarity to his voice. Don pored through his memory, trying to determine where he had heard the voice before. "Ready for what?"

"I have been sent to you by the Father. We're going to be spending some time together."

Don reeled. First, he thought he heard the very voice of God, but, surely, that was impossible. Things like that didn't happen to him. Now, a stranger had mysteriously entered the church, through a locked door, and he said they were going to spend some time together. "Who are you?" Don questioned, cautiously.

"I'm the Revealer. The Father told you I was coming."

Don sized him up, staring at the man's brown leather loafers, which looked like they could have been purchased at J.C. Penney, and moved up to his faded blue jeans and his tucked-in, button-down blue dress shirt. The man's face resembled many others. He was not unattractive, just a regular guy.

"Why are you here?" More questions kept rising in Don's mind.

"You asked the Father to let you know what is in the hearts of other people, so that's what I am going to do," the Revealer responded.

Don's eyes squinted as his eyebrows drew together. "What do you mean by 'know what is in the hearts of other people?"

"OK. You're wondering whether you really heard the Father's voice because things like that just don't happen to you. Well, it did. You did hear the Father, and He has granted you an incredible and unique gift."

Don started to shake his head. "I get it. I have finally cracked up!"

The Revealer smiled and Don noticed that, when He smiled, it seemed as if the room lit up.

"No, Don, you have not cracked up. It will make sense once I explain it."

"Wait a minute, the Father, or the Lord, or whomever I heard just a little bit ago called me Donald. You are calling me Don."

Again, the Revealer grinned.

"The Father and I are the same, but sometimes We approach matters from different angles."

"Oh, oh, oh, are you God, too?" Don's said, his eyes growing wide.

"Yes."

The calming response instantly made Don feel secure and peace surrounded him.

"But what do I call you?" Don muttered as he backed up and melted into his chair. He was, after all, having an unusual night.

"The Revealer is fine," He responded. "I'm glad you are sitting down, because we have to go over the guidelines."

Don chuckled. "Of course, there are guidelines. I mean, how often do I hear the voice of the Lord and then have a man standing in my office who is called the Revealer?"

The Revealer peered into Don's eyes, and Don noticed the captivating look that seemed to grab him. "First guideline: You are the only adult who will be able to see me."

"What do you mean, the only adult who can see you? Are you a figment of my imagination? Is this real?"

"I assure you that this is very real. Earlier this evening, you were filled with frustration and felt inadequate. You even bumped your knee into the desk. I imagine that hurt."

"It didn't feel good. Wait, how did you know that? I was alone."

A sense of comfort was conveyed by the face of the Revealer. "Don, you are never alone."

For the second time that evening, Don buried his head in his hands, hoping that when he removed them, he would be sitting there by himself, that his imagination had just played tricks on him.

After a couple of minutes, the Revealer spoke. "Don, you can't hide. Now, let's go over the guidelines. We really don't have a lot of time, just a week."

"OK, so no other adult can see You, only me, right?"

"That is correct."

Inquisitively Don snapped, "But, hey, if only I can see you and someone sees me talking to You, then they will think that I really am crazy!"

Chuckling, the Revealer answered, "The Father told me that you overthink everything. We'll communicate through thought. I know what you are thinking and I will talk to you and answer all your questions in your mind."

"So, let me get this straight," Don said, cocking his head to the side. "We're going to be together for the next week, only I will see You, and all I have to do is think and You will hear me and answer me in my head?"

The Revealer slowly nodded his head in affirmation.

Don deliberated. "Can you hear me now?"

The Revealer laughed. "Wasn't that a commercial for a cellular company years ago?" the Revealer laughed. "But the answer is 'yes.' I can hear you."

Don still wasn't convinced and wanted to test the waters. After all, he had heard the voice of God and now had the Revealer standing in front of the desk in his tiny office. Don thought, "Somewhere over the rainbow."

"We are not going to spend this week with you quoting song titles from 'The Wizard of Oz,' are we? OK. Only you will be able to see me and we'll communicate with our thoughts, but the most important guideline is that you will not be given more than you can handle, as there are some things that you do not need to know."

"I don't understand what You mean about things I can't handle or not needing to know," Don said, taken aback by the last guideline.

"Don, this is not a parlor trick or a magic show. I am going to let you know what is going on in the hearts of others around you. This is real and sensitive, and there will be times when you cannot handle it."

Don was not sure whether to be offended or appreciative, so he merely responded, "I'm not really certain what that means but I'll trust You."

The Revealer again flashed a smile that was illuminated with peace. "Yes, if you trust me, it will be much easier."

It seemed as if more and more questions started rolling like an avalanche through Don's mind. "But why me?"

The Revealer placed his hand gently on his shoulder. "Because you asked the Father and He saw fit to grant your request."

Suddenly, Don realized that he could feel the Revealer's hand on his shoulder. "I can feel your hand! Aren't you supposed to be transparent, or a hologram, or just an illusion?"

"I am everything." The Revealer's response didn't make any sense to Don, but, then, in a strange way, it made all the sense in the world.

The Revealer withdrew his hand and motioned for Don to follow him. "Let's go. We need to get you home because we have a big day tomorrow."

Thursday was the weekly meeting of the area ministers, where much posturing and preaching occurred. There usually were 15 to 20 ministers who attended, and Don wished that he could tell them that the Revealer was walking around with him.

"Oh, and by the way, you should not tell anybody that I am with you, letting you know what is in the hearts of men, because that would really cause theological train wrecks."

"I understand that because I don't understand what is going on, myself," Don said, shaking his head.

Before he turned his office lights off, Don looked around once more, because he was a different person from when he first entered the office. He was not sure how different or why he was different, he just knew that he was.

As they stood on the landing by the glass doors, Don noticed that the latch was still locked and he turned to the Revealer. "How did you get in?" He then realized the futility of his question so he thought, "Never mind."

As they exited, the Revealer remarked, "Stan is not that bad a guy and he is not really upset with Mike about his exuberant amens. He is just struggling."

Don replayed his earlier conversation with Stan and asked, "What is Stan struggling with?"

The Revealer's face cast a serious look toward Don, "Remember when I told you that I would only reveal what you needed to know?"

"Yes," Don agreed.

"This is one of those times when you do not need to know, as it is Stan's place to tell you."

Don hesitated. "But what if there are a lot of times that I don't need to know?"

The Revealer's visage returned to its usual, jovial state. "That's the way it is, and besides, many things you don't want to know."

Don accepted his clarification. "OK. Hey, how are you going to get around?" Don looked at the half-gravel, half-paved, potholed parking lot and noticed that his was the only vehicle.

"We will be together all the time, even in a car" the Revealer said.

"Do you trust my driving?" Don said.

"Much more than your cooking," the Revealer snickered.

Don didn't know whether the Revealer was teasing him or not. "What do you mean? I am a good cook!"

A smile that seemed to spread from the east to the west covered the Revealer's face. "Remember, Don. I know all things." Both laughed and walked toward Don's 15-year-old second-hand Honda Accord.

As Don gripped the handle to shut the door, he thought again about what happened tonight and wondered, why him? He had feelings of inadequacy and thought, "when I wake up in the morning, will this all be a dream caused by a weird food combination?" It seemed as if Don's mind was caught up in a tumultuous whirlwind.

"You will be all right. I am with you," the Revealer reassured him. "This week, you will learn much about other people, but you will learn more about yourself."

Don grabbed the seatbelt and clicked it into place. "I think I understand that, but I'm a little nervous about this experience."

The Revealer's eyes seemed to bore right into Don's soul. It was not a menacing, scary feeling, but one of compassion. "Please know that the Father and I would never harm you or lead you where you were not supposed to be. You have been granted this experience because it will awaken in you an intimacy with Us that you cannot begin to imagine."

"I want that closeness," Don thought, meekly.

"We know that, and that is what is going to take place this week."

"But," Don started, then abruptly stopped. It seemed that, while Don's heart was filled with peace, there was another force, another presence that continued to disrupt him, raising questions about the reality of what he was experiencing. "I know this is going to be stretching and challenging," he muttered, as if trying to convince himself.

The Revealer paused. "I know the enemy is planting thoughts into your mind right now and you are wondering how this is going to work. You are not going to understand a lot, but what you do will be liberating."

"The enemy, yes. There is a devil and he wants to stop God's work. He wants to interrupt us from knowing You. He wants to get between us!" Don exclaimed, as if it were a new thought that just popped into his head. "How come we haven't talked about the enemy until now? Shouldn't that have been one of the guidelines?"

"We don't dwell on the enemy because he has been defeated," the Revealer said. "He has no power and no authority. Remember when I told you that the Father and I approach things from different angles? There are not just two of us. We are three, the Father and the Son and Myself. The Son fulfilled His role and now He is in paradise. I am fulfilling part of My role with you, as the Revealer."

"The Trinity!" Don shouted.

"Yes, We are three but one."

"Of course, I knew that, but now it makes a lot more sense," Don burst out. "At first, I was talking to the Father, and He sent me the Revealer."

"Yes, I was promised by the Son to His followers. I am here to encourage you and to remind you what the Son accomplished."

Curiosity swirled through Don. "Will I get to talk to the Son, too?"

The Revealer shook his head to the left and right and said, "Don, you are going to have a unique experience with Me that the Father has allowed. Let's not be greedy."

"I understand. I'm just trying to wrap my head around all of this, and when I start understanding it, it doesn't make sense."

"I know, but it will one day," the Revealer replied. "For this next week, just receive the lessons that I will be teaching you and don't overthink it."

"It must be written in Heaven somewhere: Don Stout, the overthinker," Don said.

Joining him in laughter, the Revealer said, "Remember, it is important to have your name written in Heaven. Now, let's get home."

Don twisted the key in the ignition and the motor slowly came alive. "But what if questions keep coming up this week? What happens if we spend a week together and I don't have all the questions answered? What will happen after this week is over?"

For the second time, the Revealer placed his hand on Don's shoulder. "So many concerns, so many questions. Don't worry!"

Don said, "Thank you for being patient. I know that this is a great honor, I just don't get it. One last question: Will you wear a seat belt?"

The Revealer snickered. "Remember, Don, only you can see me. What would happen if we were driving and someone looked in and saw a seatbelt pulled away from the seat?"

"Good point." Don laughed with the Revealer. Slowly, with only Don buckled in, he pulled out of the small church parking lot, avoiding the potholes, and drove to the parsonage.

TWO

As he accelerated gently up the slanted driveway of the parsonage, Don was not quite sure what to do. His first impulse was to madly sprint in to tell his wife everything, but would that be wise? Don wondered, "How much should I share with my wife? How much should she know?"

The Revealer told Don, "Tell your wife what you would like to tell her. She is your greatest supporter."

Don realized that the Revealer knew every one of his thoughts and replied, "That's right. You're not only going to let me know about everyone else's heart, but You know mine as well."

As they approached the parsonage, covered in brown and white siding with a cheery wreath on the beige door, Don was grateful his family had a nice place to live. They couldn't afford otherwise to live in a comparable house so early in his ministry. "Welcome to my humble home," Don said as he opened the door.

The parsonage had been built by the church 30 years ago and even though there was some wear and tear, it was still a good home. The church had endured three debt campaigns and was proud that it had retired the mortgage and the house was paid off. This had occurred 10 years before Don became the pastor and the church had celebrated with a pitch-in dinner at the parsonage. Those attending had been very careful not to stain the new shag carpeting.

The three-bedroom, 1,500-square-foot house contained a full basement, which at one time had been used for a fellowship hall when a failed sump pump caused a flood that ruined the downstairs carpet in the church. The church members had been thankful for the foresight to place a basement in the home.

The master bedroom was not huge, but it had adequate space, with a small bathroom tucked in a corner. This gave Don and his wife some privacy when they were trying to prepare for church activities and provided a brief escape when the kids got on their nerves. Each of the kids had a bedroom and the bathroom was across the hallway.

A small living room connected to the even smaller dining room, but it allowed them to all be together at mealtime. The kitchen was lined with oak cabinets that had been built by some of the members of the church, and when people visited, they made sure to show Don which of the skilled handiwork was theirs. The parsonage was not a mansion, but it was home, and Don felt blessed to live there.

Don and the Revealer stood in the entryway. As Don bent over, taking off his shoes, he noticed that the Revealer removed his brown loafers as well. "Please make yourself comfortable," Don said.

"Thank you," the Revealer said. "I will!"

The entryway was the beginning of a long hallway, with the bedrooms and the kids' bathroom branching off from it. From the entryway, a right turn led to the kitchen, where Debbie, Don's wife, was washing dishes at the sink. A left turn from the entryway led into the small dining and living room, where it sounded as if the kids were galloping around a racetrack.

When the kids heard Don enter, he was instantly mobbed by four little hands. Their oldest child, Erin, was 6 years old and too smart for her own good. She was a miniature model of Debbie, with long brown hair and a cute dimple on her right cheek. The runaway freight train was their 4-year-old, Nathaniel, who charged full-speed ahead at all times. One of his greatest joys in life was trying to pull his sister's long brown braids, but she was quite sly about staying out of his reach.

The kids grabbed each of Don's legs and tightly wrapped themselves around him. "I love my kids," he thought.

The Revealer looked at him. "Yes, they are a wonderful gift from God."

Nathaniel multitasked, gripping Don's leg and trying to swat his sister, but she stayed just out of the reach of his tiny wingspan. Don bent down and said, "OK, kids, I have to go find Mommy," and they reluctantly released their prized captive.

As they let go, the kids stared right at the Revealer. "You told me that only I can see You," Don thought.

"I told you that you were the only *adult* who could see me. Children possess a spiritual depth that allows them to see much more than adults," the Revealer corrected him.

Don's head snapped toward Erin when she pointed at the Revealer and asked, "Daddy, who is that?"

Don didn't know what to say so he paused and then slowly said, "He's . . . my . . . friend."

"He is a nice man," Erin said.

Nathaniel's head bounced up and down and he said, "nice man," and then tried to pull his sister's braid as they raced off toward the living room.

"What am I going to tell them?" Don asked the Revealer with concern. "They know You are here."

"They know more about the spiritual world than you think they do," the Revealer said with no surprise in his voice. "Sadly, as people grow up and gain worldly knowledge, they lose wisdom and allow things to cloud their sight of the spiritual realm."

"This isn't a problem?" Don said, his voice raised a notch in spite of his effort to control it.

"Not for Me, it isn't. How about you?" the Revealer said evenly.

At that time, Debbie's voice rang out. "Honey, is that you? You're a little late."

Don's eyes grew wide. "If she only knew!"

Don had met Debbie during their sophomore year at Anderson University in Anderson, Indiana. His plan had been to finish his Biblical studies program and then enter seminary. He believed that once he graduated from seminary he would be prepared for the ministry. Debbie had been studying early childhood education and wanted to teach one day.

It would be nice to say that, when they first connected, it had been love at first sight for both of them, but that wasn't accurate. When Don first caught a glimpse of Debbie at Chapel in Reardon Auditorium, he was smitten and wanted to get to know her. But she left quickly with a group of friends and Don had to shift to detective mode to discover who this beautiful woman was.

Debbie was very attractive, with long brown hair that shimmered in the sunlight. Her light green eyes sparkled as she spoke and when she smiled, a small dimple showed on her right cheek, which accentuated her soft beauty. Debbie had been very athletic, playing tennis and taking good care of herself physically.

Don was not a bad-looking guy. He was 5 feet, 10 inches tall and had played football and wrestled in high school, though he participated only in intramural sports in college. A serious student, he had not dated many girls. He had high standards, since he believed a future pastor's wife had to be special.

Don's investigative diligence paid off when he found that Debbie was a sophomore who lived in Gaston Hall and studied education. The next week after his initial discovery, he lay in wait for her after the Chapel service concluded. When she walked by, Don approached her and said, "You know, it takes a special person to be a pastor's wife."

When Debbie smiled, she glowed, displaying her unpretentious prettiness. "Yes, it does. Good luck finding one!" And she walked off.

Don was stunned. He didn't know whether he should have chased after her, recouped his loss, or burst into wailing tears. Later, Don confessed to Debbie that she ripped out his heart that day. She grinned and answered, "I know."

But Don refused to give up and continued to be "coincidentally" in the same places as Debbie. Don even thought that he caught her looking at him a few times, but he suspected that might be wishful thinking. Finally, Debbie gave Don an ounce of hope and approached him in the student center before class. "We sure are seeing each other a lot," she said. "Would you like to eat lunch at the cafeteria together sometime?"

At first, Don's vocal cords seized and all he could do was stare at her like he was a lost puppy dog. After what seemed to him an eternity, Don answered, in the deepest octave he could muster, "Yes, that would be great. We can go now and eat lunch."

Debbie laughed. "We could, I imagine, but we might want to wait until lunch time. It's only 9 o'clock in the morning."

Don regained his composure. "I know that, but I wanted to make sure that you knew that. Yes, how about lunch today?"

"It's a date then," Debbie said, and turned to go to her next class.

Don waved as she left and he didn't know whether he should jump up and down, act cool or start screaming, "We're going on a date!" Thankfully, he chose to maintain his usual demeanor and went to his first class. It was almost an act of futility, since Don could not concentrate and rehearsed endless conversations in his head. Occasionally, the name Augustine broke through the thoughts of what he wanted to say to Debbie, but that was the extent of what he retained in class that day.

Don arrived early at the cafeteria for lunch and, as Debbie approached, all he could do was grin. She smiled as they filled their trays with cellophane-packaged food and he stepped in front of her at the cashier to pay. When they arrived at the table, Don wanted to demonstrate his chivalry, but, as he went to pull out a chair for her, he bumped into his tray and spilled his drink.

Debbie laughed, but had caught the point of his well-meant gesture and was pleased. Even though Don had rehearsed countless conversations in his mind, he found himself at a loss for words. Debbie filled in the gap by asking how he knew he had been called into the ministry, and about his dreams. Their first date went quickly; both of them had afternoon classes.

As they spent more time together, Don settled down and Debbie was able to see his sweet nature and admire his walk with God. Debbie had always known the Lord; she had been saved during a church camp at an early age and was looking for a Christian husband. She was not enthusiastic about marrying a pastor, but wanted to pursue God's will for her life.

Don knew she was a little hesitant, but he slowly won her heart. They dated exclusively by the end of their junior year of college and made wedding plans after they graduated. Debbie's parents were not as excited as she was, because they knew Don was going straight into seminary, but they loved their daughter and wanted to be supportive.

Two months after Don and Debbie walked across the stage to receive their diplomas, they were married. They planned to wait to have children after Don graduated from seminary and was pastoring a church, but one night of passion altered their plans. During Don's third year of seminary, Erin joined the family. Nathaniel followed right before they were installed as the pastoral family of the church in Huron.

Time passed quickly since the little Stout family was formed and now Don and the Revealer stepped into the kitchen, Debbie's back was turned to them as she finished the dishes. Don wrapped his arms around her arms and nuzzled her neck for a soft kiss.

Debbie leaned back into his arms.

"Oh, my, someone is friendly this evening! How did Bible Study go? We weren't able to go because Nathaniel had a slight fever earlier. You can tell he is OK now because he's chasing his sister!"

"That's OK. It was the regular Bible Study. I asked what they thought that Paul meant in the text, and they talked about how it's colder than normal."

Debbie felt her husband's frustration. "I know. Hang in there."

Don released his embrace and gently shifted Debbie to face him.

"I have to tell you something. And it's big."

As Debbie turned, she dried her hands on a dish towel. "Is it good news?"

"Yes, more than yes. I mean, well I'm not sure what I mean, but God talked to me tonight."

Debbie smiled. "Yes, God spoke through you. You are His messenger."

Don shook his head. "No, I mean, God *really* spoke to me tonight."

Debbie stopped drying her hands. "OK. Where did God speak to you?"

"At the church, in my office. First, it started shaking, but it wasn't, then it was filled with smoke, but it wasn't smoke, and then I heard God."

Debbie felt Don's forehead and muttered to herself, "Maybe he has what Nathaniel had earlier."

Don softly took hold of his wife's arms. "No, I heard God's voice!"

"Was it audible? What did He sound like? What did He say?"

Don steered Debbie to sit down at the kitchen table, they had purchased at Goodwill. "His voice was audible, but it wasn't."

Debbie's brow was furrowed. "Don, you know that you are really not making any sense right now?"

"I was really frustrated after Bible Study," he continued.

Debbie lovingly clasped his hands. "I know you've been frustrated, honey."

Don pulled away. He wanted her to know that he was not making this up. "I told God that I wanted to know what was in the hearts of others."

"So how did He answer you?" Debbie asked.

"He sent the Revealer to me."

Debbie searched the eyes of her husband and thought to herself, "He looks well."

"She thinks you are sick," the Revealer told Don in a humorous tone.

Don's head perked up. "There, did you hear that?"

Debbie cautiously looked around. "Did I hear what?"

"That! The Revealer told me that you think I'm sick."

"You're the only one who can hear me," the Revealer said to Don.

"Honey, I didn't hear anything," Debbie replied patiently.

"The Revealer told me what you were thinking," Don tried to explain.

Debbie truly tried to understand what her husband meant. "Why would the Revealer tell you what I was thinking?"

"Because that's what I asked God for," he answered with slight annoyance in his tone. "I want to know what is in the hearts of others."

"Why would you do that, sweetheart?" Debbie asked, her face filled with curiosity.

"Because I think it will help me to know how to help others grow closer to God and, besides, I will probably grow as well," Don said.

"So, this Revealer, is He God, too?" She was Don's No. 1 supporter and she wanted to help him.

Don started to smile. "Yes, He is God."

"Then, honey, anytime you are growing closer to God, I support that," she said.

"So, do you believe me?" Don asked.

"Honey, I believe that you want to grow closer to God, and that's one of the many reasons why I love you." As she smiled, her signature dimple appeared on her right cheek.

The Revealer interjected. "You know that she's right. One of the reasons the Father granted you this gift is to deepen your walk with Him."

Don responded audibly, "I know that." Then he realized all he had to do was think, and the Revealer would know what he was thinking.

Debbie turned around. "I'm glad to know that you know how much I love you!" She walked over and kissed him. Then she turned and said, "Oh, it's your night to tuck in the kids. I'll start corralling them to their rooms."

Don stared straight ahead. "That went well."

"What did you expect?"

"I thought she would completely believe me and that somehow, some way, she could hear You."

"Debbie always listens to Me, but in a much different manner than you are right now," the Revealer said.

"But wouldn't it make it easier if she could hear You like I hear You?" Don shook his head.

The Revealer responded, "No," the Revealer responded. "We meet people where they are. At this point in your life, you asked the Father for a gift that will help you, and this is how the Father provided it."

Don clasped his forehead. "The more I understand about this situation, the more I don't understand!"

"Now, you are starting to get it!" the Revealer said. "You don't have to figure it out. You just have to believe."

Don replied in resignation, "Help my unbelief."

"That's what this week is all about."

Just then, loud giggles arose from a rambunctious stampede in the hallway. "Honey, the kids are going to their rooms and they are waiting for Daddy," Debbie said.

"I'll be there in a minute," Don called out. He turned to the Revealer and asked, "Are you going with me?"

The Revealer smirked. "Oh, yeah. I wouldn't miss this for the world."

"I'm warning You: It might take all Your strength," Don joked.

"Don't worry! We love children," the Revealer said, joining Don as he turned down the hallway to go into Nathaniel's room.

The wallpaper in the room was plastered with Paw Patrol and lots of big and little colorful dogs with their tongues hanging out, staring at all those who were in the room. Nathaniel bounced on his bed playfully.

"Now, buddy, we talked about how you are not supposed to do that," Don reminded his son.

Nathaniel leaped one more time and looked at his Dad. "Why not?"

Don grabbed him, wrapped him in his arms and started tickling him. "Because this is what can happen!" They wrestled playfully for a few minutes.

"I imagine this technique will settle him down quickly," the Revealer teased.

From the end of the hallway, Debbie's voice called out. "You boys had better not be wrestling. It's time for bed!" Nathaniel's eyes widened as his Dad whispered, "We're going to get into trouble." They both snickered again.

Trying to settle Nathaniel down, Don said, "OK, it's time to get under the covers. We'll read a Bible story and pray, then go to sleep."

Nathaniel climbed under his multicolored Superman blanket, while Don grabbed a thin book from the bookshelf. "Oh, this is a good one. It's about Jonah and the whale."

"I like that one!" Nathaniel squealed.

"I do, too." the Revealer said.

Don wondered whether Nathaniel could hear him, since he could see the Revealer, but Nathaniel did not appear to notice that anything had been said.

"There was a preacher named Jonah, who was told by God to go to a place called Nineveh and preach to them," Don read from the book.

"Isn't that what you do, Daddy?" Nathaniel asked.

"Yes, it is, but I hope that I always do what God wants me to do," Don said. glancing over at the Revealer.

Don continued to read. "But Jonah did not want to go and ran away by getting on a boat. But the boat started to break down and Jonah was thrown into the sea and swallowed by a whale."

"I don't think that would be fun," Nathaniel remarked.

"Oh, the wisdom of children," the Revealer said. Don understood his point, but then became curious, and thought of a question for the Revealer.

"If you are going to tell me what is in the hearts of people, what's in Nathaniel's heart right now?"

"Exactly what you see," the Revealer said. "He is pure. He knows that getting swallowed by a whale would not be fun."

"That's it? That's what his heart is saying?"

"I told you, Don, adults complicate things while children accept. That's why you have to become childlike to enter into the Kingdom of Heaven."

Don nodded and continued aloud. "But then, Jonah was spit out by the whale onto land," he said and he grabbed Nathaniel, tickling him.

"Then Jonah went to Nineveh and preached, and they were saved," Don said, finishing the story.

Nathaniel pulled his covers to his neck. "That's a good story, Daddy," Nathaniel said, pulling his covers to his neck. "We want people to be saved, don't we?"

His eyes moist, Don replied, "Yes, we do. Now, let's pray."

Nathaniel pulled his little hands out from under the blankets and grasped them together. "Is your friend going to pray with us, too?"

"Yes, I'm sure He is going to join us," Don said and prayed for his son.

As they were walking to Erin's room, Don stopped. "Is Erin's heart as pure as Nathaniel's?"

"Yes, she has the faith of her mother," the Revealer assured him.

Erin's room was a conglomeration of Barbie dolls and toy ponies. Her dolls were all set up on one side of the room, having tea together, while a collection of long-maned ponies stood nearby. She was already under her covers, patiently waiting for her father.

"Was he jumping on his bed?" she asked.

"Yes, he was." Don smiled.

"Boys!" Erin responded exasperated.

"Honey, what story would you like tonight?" Don asked.

Erin's eyes brightened. "The one about Queen Esther. I think she had a lot of ponies."

The Revealer told Don, "She's right," the Revealer told Don. "They know."

Don caught himself feeling pride in his kids, but also a little jealous that they seemed to be so close to God. Don described how Esther became the queen and then risked her life to save God's people.

"I love that story!" Erin said. "She could have been hurt, but she didn't want others to be hurt, did she Daddy? And we don't want others to hurt, either."

Again, Don felt his eyes tear up. "No, honey, we don't want others to hurt as well."

"She's getting old enough to recognize when others are hurting and she's sensitive and feels compassion toward them," The Revealer said.

Erin started to play with her fingers. "Daddy, can I ask you a question?"

"Sure, honey, anything at all."

"There is a girl in my class, but she's always sad. I feel bad for her. Can we pray for her?" Erin, who had just started first grade, asked her father.

Don looked at the Revealer, then answered Erin. "Yes, we can. Is there anything else you want to pray for?"

"Can I pray about having a real pony?" she giggled.

Don smothered her with kisses. "Lord, thank you for my daughter and thank you for her heart to pray for her friend at school. Help her friend, please, and, Lord, help my heart to feel the same way."

The Revealer joined with them and echoed, "Amen."

There was one last hug and kiss. As they left the room, Erin said, "Good-night, sir. I hope that you have fun with my Dad." She turned toward the wall and snuggled deeper into her fluffy blankets, which were covered with pink ponies.

The Revealer looked at Don and quoted Matthew 5:8: "Blessed are the pure in heart for they shall see God."

Debbie almost ran over Don in the hallway. "I have to go to the basement to bring up the extra leaf for the table," she said. "Remember we're having people over for supper on Saturday night."

"I'll go get it," Don offered. "Oh, who's coming over?"

"The Moffits," Debbie said. "I told you that Eldene stopped by today, didn't I?"

"No. What did she want?"

Eldene Moffit and her husband, Lowell, had attended the church for many years. Lowell was a quiet, unassuming, hard-working cattle farmer with thick, calloused hands as a result of raising hundreds of steers. Eldene was gruff and didn't hesitate to share her opinion. But when the tough exterior was peeled away, it revealed a heart of gold. She would visit the parsonage and complain about how "dirty" the kitchen cabinets were, and then quickly disappear to her car.

Shortly after her departure, she and Lowell would return with brown paper sacks of groceries and choice cuts of meat that had been slaughtered on their small ranch. It took Don and Debbie a few times before they realized that Eldene wasn't "searching" their cupboards for dust, but was checking to see what they needed and then returning to fill the cabinets with food. Lowell always grinned at Don as he carried bulging bag after bag of food into the house and, being a man of few words, spoke wisely, "Better not get in the way of Eldene's dusting!"

Debbie continued her explanation of Saturday night's plans. "It was just Eldene's regular grocery checkup, and she invited them over to dinner on Saturday, but they're bringing the food. You know how they take care of us, but they don't want us to know what they are doing."

As Don headed to the basement the Revealer said, "You can tell what is in the hearts of some people, like the Moffits, by their actions."

"True," Don laughed. "But we were sure surprised the first time that she came to the house complaining about how dirty the inside of the freezer was only to return and stock it with two months' worth of meat."

"When you see the heart—the true heart—of others, it will help you to minister to them and it will help you to see your own."

They returned from the basement with the table extension and Don placed it into place. "Thank you for getting that," Debbie said. "I'm going to bed now."

"I won't be long."

Now it was just Don and the Revealer standing in the tiny dining room. "What's in Debbie's heart?" Don asked.

The Revealer breathed deeply. "Her heart is filled with the love of God and her love for you. At times, she gets overwhelmed because of your frustration, but she would never allow you to know that."

"Why not?" Don snapped, defensively.

"That is the nature of love. You know 1 Corinthians 13, love is patient, it is kind . . ."

"Yes, I know, but she can tell me anything, I don't want her heart to hurt." Don found himself feeling inadequate.

The Revealer gazed hard at Don. "There, you are internalizing your own feelings of inadequacy instead of knowing her heart and how to help her. When you learn the heart of others, it will help you to provide what they need."

Don felt chastised but knew the Revealer was right and tried to shift the focus from himself. "What if I want to help someone, but they don't want help?"

"We are to be the light and salt for others, but if they reject that, then we continue to minister to them. The ultimate choice is up to them. It is the same for you, Don. Do you really want to know what is in the hearts of others without making it an issue of your heart?"

Don knew the question hit home. "Will you help me to focus on the hearts of others this week?"

"Absolutely. You can learn from your wife, as well. Her heart beats for others. Mothers, Godly women, and Godly wives are a special gift to humanity."

Don nodded his head. "I need to pay closer attention to her heart and let her know how much I appreciate her."

"Now we're in agreement. It's easy for humans to criticize and complain and point out what another is doing wrong, but it's much more difficult to honor and respect and lift each other up," the Revealer said wistfully.

"Thank you," Don said. "I don't think I'm getting all of this, but I'm getting some."

"That is why you were chosen; you are willing to learn."

"And I have so much to learn," Don said humbly.

"Every person has much to learn and I will teach, if you will receive," the Revealer said.

The Revealer walked to the entryway and began putting his shoes on.

"Wait a minute," Don said. "I thought that you were going to stay with me all week."

The Revealer straightened up. "I am not leaving. I will never leave you, but you need to go to your wife and let her know how much you love and appreciate her."

Don smiled. "Yes, I do." He started toward their bedroom and slowly opened the door. "Honey, are you still up?"

She had been reading a devotional and placed it aside. "Yes, is everything all right?

Don affectionately looked at her. "I'm sorry that I haven't appreciated your heart. I want you to know that I'm going to do better with that."

Debbie cocked her head to the side. "You are full of surprises tonight."

Don paused. "I really want you to know that I love you, and I love how you love me and the kids and God."

Debbie's eyes teared up. "Don, I love you with all of my heart."

"I know that you do," he said, and then playfully pounced on the bed. He grabbed his wife and grinned. "Is it OK if I wrestle with you?"

And they had a good night.

THREE

The chorus of "I Can Only Imagine" was softly emanating from Don's alarm-clock radio at 6:30 a.m., so he stirred to get out of bed. He had a full day planned, with a ministers' meeting and then visits to the hospital and nursing home in Bedford. Sitting at the edge of his bed, he glanced at his wife, still resting.

Don thought to himself, "Well I'm not sure what happened last night, but it seems as if I imagined a lot of things." Suddenly, he was startled by a soft rapping on his bedroom door. Wondering if it was one of the kids, he rose and walked toward it. When he arrived at the door, he whispered, "Shh, Mommy is still sleeping."

The Revealer responded, "I know. I'm here for you. Get ready. We have a big day today."

It was then that Don realized that what happened last night was real. He was going to spend a week with the Revealer and learn what is in the hearts of those he met. "Yes, last night did happen, so let's go," the Revealer gently admonished.

Don showered, dressed, and went out to the kitchen, where the Revealer was standing. "I'm going to have some coffee and head to the church to do a little paperwork before the ministerial meeting."

"I know," the Revealer replied.

After two pieces of buttered toast and a cup and a half of coffee, Don looked at the Revealer. "I'm ready," he said, and when they entered the hallway, a tiny figure in pony-covered pajamas appeared outside of her bedroom. "Bye, Daddy, I love you," Erin whispered as she waved her little hand.

"Bye-bye, honey. Have a good day at school, and I love you, too," Don said.

Smiling, Erin waved again and said, "Bye, sir. Have fun with Daddy today." The Revealer's face sweetly beamed toward her and He lifted His hand to wave at her.

As they left the house, Don turned to the Revealer and said, "I'm amazed at how the kids can see you."

"Don't be, Don," the Revealer said. "Those who have eyes to see will see."

"I wonder how good my vision is?" Don pondered, introspectively.

The Revealer looked at him. "You are only beginning to see."

When they arrived at the church, Don unlocked the door and they headed toward his office. As Don opened the office door, he said, "Here is where everything started. It will be interesting to see how it unfolds."

The Revealer warmly assured him, "It will unfold according to how the Father wants it to unfold, to work for your good."

Don's face scrunched up a little. "You know, that's a scripture verse that I never truly understood."

"Romans 8:28, God works all things out for the good of those who love Him."

"Yes, how did you know which one I was talking about? Never mind. It's going to take me a while to remember that You know what I am thinking."

The Revealer smiled.

"But what about when bad things happen to me and others?" Don continued. "What about when we think everything is going to be all right, but it all goes wrong?"

Don started thinking about the many people with whom he prayed who were not healed, and the many situations he faced that seemed to continue to slide into worse circumstances.

"It's like putting a giant jigsaw puzzle together, but you can't see what the picture looks like or is supposed to be," the Revealer said.

"But wouldn't it be much easier if we knew in the very beginning what it was supposed to look like?" Don asked.

The Revealer sat on the corner of Don's desk. "Don, each event or act in your life happens for a reason. It takes place to teach you a lesson. If you knew everything from the very beginning, you wouldn't learn through the process."

"The process? What do you mean, the process?"

"The process of becoming the person you are supposed to be, the building of your faith, and strengthening of your relationship with the Father."

"But what does that have to do with a jigsaw puzzle?" Don thought.

"Each event, act, or situation you go through, no matter how insignificant or minor you perceive it to be, offers you a lesson to learn more about the Father."

Don moved over to his chair and sat down. "And when we put them all together, we can start to see the bigger picture, the puzzle."

The Revealer smiled. "You are starting to get it now. That means even hard times, hurtful circumstances, painful points in your life are not the big, overall total picture. They are each just one piece. When you put them all together, the Father is working everything out for your good."

Don mused, "I had not thought about it that way. I guess that we people only concentrate on the individual piece we are holding in our hand instead of the complete picture that God has."

"Yes, and that is faith. Faith is knowing that there are many pieces and some pieces that were difficult to fit into the puzzle before now are there so you'll be able to piece more and more together," the Revealer said.

"You know, it would be a lot easier if You and the Father just wrote everything out for us," Don quipped.

"We have. It's in the Bible."

Don laughed. "I should have known that was coming. Well, in a couple of hours we're going to hear a lot about the Bible and many opinions about every verse."

It was now the Revealer's turn to laugh. "You're talking about the ministers' meeting. There are times that the Father wonders, 'How did they come up with that interpretation?'"

A serious look came over Don's face. "I imagine there are times when we people really disappoint You and the Father."

The Revealer seemed saddened. "More than you know."

Don stood up and momentarily wanted to wrap his arms around the Revealer, but then didn't know if it was allowed. "I'm sorry. So why are You and the Father so good to us unruly people?'

The Revealer smiled. "Because We love you."

Don sat back down and felt a warming presence fill his office, not because the thermostat was operating, but because he was in the presence of a loving God.

The arrowed hands of the clock on the wall now pointed to 10 a.m. and Don said, "The ministers' meeting starts at 10:30, so we need to get going."

The Revealer said, "I know."

Driving in the car, they passed over the bumpy railroad tracks leading out of town and headed along State Route 50, journeying toward Bedford. It was autumn and the countless trees surrounding Huron were shifting from their normal green leafy covering to brilliant hues of many colors.

Following the curvy road, Don and the Revealer were hemmed in on both sides by radiant red, awe-striking yellow and gorgeous orange foliage, which shouted of the creativity of the Father.

Don was taking in the breathtaking scenery and said, "You know, the Father made some great landscape."

The Revealer nodded His head. "I was there."

Don looked at Him with admiration. As they turned into Bedford and passed the Dairy Queen, Don saw the Bedford First Church of God. It was one of the larger churches in town; about 400 people attended its Sunday morning services. The pastor, Jerry Liddle, was a good man, but an older one, who kept thinking and rethinking the date of his retirement.

Jerry and Don had breakfast together once a month at a local hometown restaurant in Bedford called Bob's. After Don finished his regular bacon-and-sausage omelet, he and Jerry discussed questions that Don had compiled since their last meeting. Don appreciated their conversations and always learned something from his more seasoned and experienced mentor that he could apply practically to his life and ministry.

After their meetings, they would return to the church and Don would walk up and down among the beige-covered chairs in the sanctuary, which was much larger than his. Often, he wished that one day he would have a church as big as Bedford First. Jerry knew Don did this, but would merely return to his office to leave his younger, ambitious protégé to himself.

Today, in the Hospitality Room of the church, there were two long, rectangular tables set up with about 20 chairs. Of course, there was a table in the corner filled with boxes of fresh chocolate-covered donuts next to several carafes of coffee and one ignored pitcher filled with apple juice. There was always a small fruit tray on the table as well, which held cut-up pieces of apples, oranges, and melons. It did not receive the attention the baked, sugary, doughnuts did.

Even though the meeting was supposed to begin at 10:30, most of the ministers started straggling in at about 10:40. Sometimes, Don wondered whether it was to one-up each other, to show how busy each of them was and how much they had to do. Don was always early because he wanted to drop into Jerry's office and say "hello." The meetings usually kicked off about 10:45, after the whirlwind of late arrivals, handshaking, and looking around to see who was going to sit by whom finally settled down.

Don and the Revealer walked through the entryway by way of the large wooden double doors leading to the narthex area, which was a substantial room where people greeted each other and milled around before and after services. There were several television monitors hanging on the walls, which scrolled through the announcements of the church repeatedly. If they had turned to the right from the narthex, they would have walked into the sanctuary, with which Don was familiar.

Instead, they continued walking straight and took a left toward Jerry's office. Don popped his head inside the door and greeted the church secretary. She was a sweet woman, who smiled and called out, "Pastor Liddle, that young minister is here to see you." Don was not sure whether she knew his name because she always addressed him as "that young minister."

Jerry walked out of his office, putting on his stylish blue suit coat and smiled. "He's not here to see me. He's here for the meeting. You know, he is the man of the hour. He is leading our devotional time this morning."

Don almost fainted as he remembered being assigned to lead this month's devotional time. It was a 15-minute block of time, and a short discussion generally followed during which many of the ministers contributed and shared their viewpoints. Sadly, many times the devotion leaders only wanted to demonstrate how erudite and Biblically knowledgeable they were since they desired to impress their colleagues. There was an unspoken competition about who could lead the most spiritual and effective devotion.

Don heard the voice of the Revealer in his head. "You forgot that you were leading the devotion this morning, didn't you?"

"Yes!" Don replied. "I was going to prepare it last night after the Bible study, but then You and the Father showed up and I got sidetracked!"

The Revealer grinned. "I'm sure I can help you with it if you want me to."

"Want you to help me? Yes, that would be very nice of You," Don said sarcastically.

Jerry extended his hand, warmly shook Don's hand and said, "I'm looking forward to hearing what you have to share this morning."

"Me, too!" Don said.

Don, the Revealer, and Jerry laughed and then walked toward the Hospitality Room, just a few doors away from the office. As they entered, there were only seven other ministers present. Most of them were holding chocolate-covered donuts smothered with caramel icing and cups of coffee. Don quickly headed to the coffee and thought, "Maybe a dose of caffeine will give me a devotion."

The Revealer said to him, "Maybe I will give you the devotion."

Don paused. "Yeah, that would be a good idea."

It was 10:43 and most of the ministers were settling down and finding their seats at the tables. Sixteen ministers were able to attend the meeting today and there would be much wondering and surmising about the reasons why the others did not attend. The longer the hushed conversations continued, the juicier the stories grew about why someone was not present.

Every year, the ministers elected a president of their ministerial alliance through a ratification process. Names would be tossed out like loose confetti and then each person nominated merely smiled, shook their head negatively, and offered another name. The ministers chose not to pursue leadership in the alliance because everyone knew that Pastor Harold Brunn wanted the position.

Harold had lived in Bedford for 22 years, two years longer than Jerry. He remembered every past event, function, or member of the ministerial alliance and was quick to share his knowledge. He had pastored for 38 years, starting when he was 24 years old, so he and Jerry were considered the senior ministers.

Harold was the minister at the tall-steepled First Christian Church, which had the highest attendance in the area, a fact that was shared loudly and proudly. Harold was not as narcissistic as one might think after first meeting him, and actually was extremely insecure. With the culture of the world rapidly changing around him, and even the culture of the church transforming, he was merely treading water to keep afloat.

Harold's voice bellowed as he called the meeting to order, and then delivered an eloquent prayer, which he may or may not have practiced many times before. Following his usual lengthy prayer, a chorus of sanctimonious "amens" echoed around the white plastic tables.

This morning, as Harold was wrapping up his homily disguised as a prayer, Don thought, "I wonder what is in his heart?"

The Revealer responded with a question. "Why do you ask?"

Don tried not to appear nosy or rude. "I just thought that's why we are spending time together this week."

"Don't be falsely humble," the Revealer mildly chastised. "Remember, I always know what's going on in your heart. When Harold first started in the ministry, he was a lot like you. You have many characteristics that mirror each other."

"What? There's no way! He knows it all and thinks he's a big shot because he has the largest church."

The Revealer did not ease up on Don. "Don't be too quick to judge and don't assume you would act differently in the same situation."

Don seemed confused. "What situation?"

"Pastor Brunn did not always serve in a large church. He started with a much smaller congregation. After a few years, he moved to a larger church, but then had significant problems with his leadership. Some in the congregation were immoral and he didn't know how to handle it, so they attacked him and his family and ran them out of the church."

"I never knew any of this," Don said with sincere sympathy.

"No, no you didn't. That's why you need to know people's hearts. Pastor Brunn does come off in an irritating manner because he has built a thick wall to protect his heart. He believes that when others know how much he knows; they will think that he is in control. After he and his family were wounded so deeply at his second church, he made a conscious decision that he, and only he, would be in control."

"But what about the Father being in control?" Don retorted.

"What about the times that you have tried to be in more control than the Father?" the Revealer rebuked Don.

Don's eyes glanced downward. "You're right. I'm sorry."

"Now for our devotion," boomed the ostentatious voice of Harold, and he glanced over at Don. Harold was taken aback momentarily because when he saw Don it was as if Don was looking straight into his soul and assuring him that God loved him.

"Thank you, Pastor Brunn. I want to say thank you to all of our wiser and more experienced pastors because, sometimes, we younger ones think we know everything, but we need to learn more."

The Revealer nodded his head. "Good job."

Harold thought, "Maybe that young minister respects me. I will have to spend some time with him."

With all eyes on him, Don was jolted back into reality because he was supposed to deliver a spiritual devotion, a riveting presentation that challenged, encouraged, and taught the ministers a valuable lesson. Don looked at each of them, smiled, and cried out to the Revealer, "How about a little help?"

The Revealer instantly supplied this to Don. "Imagine, if one night after you had ministered, maybe a Bible study, Sunday service, or simply ministry event, you heard the very voice of God."

Don interrupted Him. "I don't have to imagine that!"

The Revealer continued, "What would God say to you and would there be any areas in your life He would bring up to you?"

Don was quizzical. "That's my devotion?" Other ministers had examined the Greek roots of words and linguistically parsed verses emerging with great insight. Other devotions were mini sermons that inspired and uplifted the others, who sat around in agreement. Don was supposed to just ask them what would God say to them?

Plainly, in Don's head, the Revealer emphatically said, "Yes."

Don again looked at each of the ministers. "Imagine that after a ministry event or activity you could hear the actual voice of God. What do you think He would say to you? Would He affirm you? Do you think He would let you know what you needed to work on in your life?"

Some of the ministers were leaning forward in their seats, almost challenging Don to teach them something they didn't know. Others came off as if they nonchalantly bided their time through the devotion, so they could later make an announcement about an upcoming event at their church.

But Don's questions piqued their curiosity. Those who were leaning forward shifted back a little in their padded metal seats, and those who were waiting their turn to speak stared off into space, thinking of an answer.

Of course, Harold spoke first. "I hope that God would say I was doing a good job, that He was proud of me."

The Revealer prodded Don. "Hear his heart."

Harold continued, "When all is said or done, I only want God's approval."

"That's true for the most part," the Revealer told Don.

Pastor Ron Hutchins, a minister only five years older than Don, was the jokester of the group and often cut up to provide levity, sometimes when needed, sometimes inappropriately. Ron kidded, "I hope that God would say I was getting a raise."

As chuckling rose through the room, Pastor Jim Warren didn't want Ron to be wittier than he was, so he retorted, "Ron, you already make more than you should."

Again, more laughter and Don started thinking, "This devotion is a dud. All they are doing is laughing and no one is taking it seriously."

Patiently, the Revealer spoke to Don, "Wait. Their hearts are hiding behind humor. If people are laughing, then they are not looking deeper. Humor is important and necessary, but there is a time and a place."

"This is not the time or the place." Don started to become frustrated.

"Don, this is not about you. Open your heart to see the hearts of these two."

"But You are supposed to tell me what is in their hearts," Don protested.

"They are telling you, but you're not listening."

"I'm listening, but all they're doing is clowning around," Don angrily thought.

"Don't rush, Don. Remember, it's in the Father's time," the Revealer assured him.

The smirk left Ron's face and he continued, "What do you mean, if God talked to me?"

Jim, still trying to be funny, said, "It would be a short conversation because I don't have too much to work on." This comment brought eye-rolling and one minister grabbed his chest, simulating having a heart attack.

Don cut the levity short and turned to Ron. "Ron, I mean, what do you think that God would actually say to you? What if it was just the two of you, and He was speaking directly to you?"

Ron scanned the floor, almost in a hollow manner. "I hope that He would say it's going to be all right."

The other ministers stopped fidgeting and Harold gently inquired, "Ron, what do you mean?"

Ron spoke softly. "I just don't know whether I am making a difference. I just don't know if I'm a good minister."

The Revealer smoothly nudged Don. "Hear his heart."

Ron continued, "I had such big plans in the beginning of my ministry, but now it seems all I do is put out fires. All I do is referee people who have been fighting for years."

The Revealer looked intently at Ron. "Does any of this sound familiar?" Don knew what the Revealer meant and felt uncomfortable, but something seemed to be stirring.

Don began to notice the mood of the entire room shifting. There had been much backslapping, bragging, and self-deprecation as they gathered. When the devotion began, it seemed as if it was going to be a giant laugh fest, and then they would get on to the important business—their business. But now, it was as if the Holy Spirit was leading the ministers, as if they were hearing from the Father.

Don looked at the Revealer, who rose from his chair and walked around the room, transforming it from a normal meeting to one in which they felt they were standing on holy ground.

Another minister, Pastor Jack Lutz, stood up and with tears in his eyes said, "Ron, you are not the only one. Sometimes when I preach, I wonder if the people got the message. Did I do a good enough job for them to understand?"

Others were now slightly rocking in their seats and Don didn't know whether they were doing so in agreement or feeling uncomfortable.

Jerry, with a wisdom that only comes from experience, said, "Boys, when I was younger, I felt much like you right now. The Lord came to me one evening and taught me that I was not called to be successful, just obedient. When you read through the pages of the Bible, there were many people who would not have been considered successful. Moses did not even enter the Promised Land, after enduring all that grumbling and whining. Most of the Twelve Disciples were put to death in horrific manner, and even Paul experienced times of struggle. He was executed, with many of the churches that he had established failing to survive. But the point is, they were obedient. That's the issue God dealt with me so many years ago. Would I be obedient?"

The sweet words that flowed through Jerry's heart seeped into the souls of the others. Some of the ministers sat up in their seats a little taller, while others seemed to solemnly slump as they were taking an inventory of their hearts.

Ron was now smiling. "I get that. It's not about me, or whether I have my face on a highway billboard or am on a syndicated show that's broadcast from coast to coast. It's about being obedient and doing the best I can."

Jim said, "Ron, I'm sorry. I was just joking. You know I do that. Don asked what issue would God talk to me about. When I get a little edgy, I have to make a joke about it. It helps me to cope. When things get rough, I think that if I can get someone to laugh, then they won't get mad."

Ron reached over the table to his friend and briefly clasped his hands. "Jim, I love you and I love your humor. I wrestle with the same issue."

Another minister, Pastor Tom Smith, cleared his voice. "Brothers, please forgive me because there have been times when I have been critical of other ministers and other churches. God has dealt with me on this before, but now I see that we all have issues and struggles."

Pastor Dave Sessums, who had not been in the community for long, stood up and walked around the end of his table and embraced Tom and said, "On behalf of my fellow ministers, we will forgive you, if you forgive us for the times we have done the same thing."

Tom openly wept. "I forgive you." The two continued their healing embrace.

The Revealer sat among the ministers with a smile on His face and Don looked at Him. "You knew all along what these ministers needed. You knew that they needed to share their hearts."

"That's all every person wants. They want others to know their hearts. But when people have been hurt because they have shared their hearts, they put up walls and build barricades so that others can't see their hearts again." The Revealer told Don.

"Because they don't want to get hurt again."

"Yes, Don, so they won't get hurt," the Revealer said. "When you see people's hearts and can get them to lower any obstacle that they have surrounded themselves with, that's when you can really minister to them."

Don spoke to himself. "That's what people want. They want to know that they are loved."

"Yes, ministers today preach about love, teach about love, sing hymns and choruses in church about love, and counsel about love, but many people, including themselves, have not received the unconditional love of the Father."

Don's question almost came out audibly, but then he caught himself. "But why don't we people let God love us?"

The Revealer paused. "Look around. You are the ones who are supposed to know that, but many of you don't love yourself at times. Isn't that true about yourself, Don? Do you always let God love you?"

Don bowed his head and teared up. "No, I don't always let God love me." After a short interlude, it was almost as if Don woke from a coma and realized that he was supposed to be leading a devotion.

"I would like to end with letting you all know something that I wrestle with as well. God loves you," Don told the pastors. "He loves you, not because you are the most eloquent orator. He loves you, not because you have the biggest church. He loves you, not because you are the greatest leader. God loves you because you are His child."

For what seemed to be an eternity, no one spoke. Even Harold, who usually knew what to say at all times, was silent. One would think that during this moment of unusual stillness there would have been a raging awkwardness, but there was not. The ministers were in one accord, receiving the love of God. They allowed themselves not to be judged by themselves or others, not to have unrealistic expectations thrust upon them, and not to be pushed around by the enemy who seeks to discourage and destroy. They simply sat in the presence of the Revealer, who poured the Father's love upon them.

Finally, Harold interrupted the holy time. "OK. Now is there any business we need to discuss?" Normally, there would have been posturing to make sure that every event was announced for a show-and-tell session of "look at what we are doing." But that was not the case today. The ministers looked around at each other, smiled, and enjoyed each other's company.

After a few short obligatory remarks, Harold motioned toward Don. "Young man, that was a powerful devotion that allowed us all to spend some time growing closer to the Lord. Thank you for that. Would you close us in prayer?"

Don had never been asked to close the ministers' meeting in prayer and was stunned. "Wow, I'm not sure what to say."

"Tell them that God loves them, bless them, and then say 'Amen,'" the Revealer instructed.

As the meeting ended, Don observed several ministers huddling together as they ministered to one another.

When Ron and Jim were leaving, they kidded, "Not a bad devotion for a new guy. Keep working on it, and you'll be all right." They both laughed.

Jerry asked Don if he would accompany him back to his office and Don said "sure."

They walked back quietly and when they entered Jerry's office, he closed the door and took off his suit coat. "Don, you seem to be growing in the Lord, which is a good thing. Is there anything going on?"

Don laughed. "Let's just say this was not an empty devotion for me. God has been talking to me."

Jerry eased into the brown leather chair behind his organized desk. "I'm glad to hear that. Someday, I look forward to hearing what He has been saying to you."

"And I will be happy to share with you." Then, they both stood and joined in a hug of encouragement.

As Don and the Revealer walked toward his car, Don stopped. "Thank you."

The Revealer peered into Don's eyes. "You are welcome. Thank you for being obedient."

They climbed into Don's car and drove to the hospital where Don made weekly visits.

FOUR

While driving to Bedford Memorial Hospital, Don glanced at the Revealer as if he wanted to say something, but remained silent. The Revealer knew exactly what Don was thinking, but most times He gave people the opportunity to make the first move. There were times when the Revealer initiated the connection and other times when the Revealer spoke so loudly it was almost as if He was barging through a loud metal door. But He waited for Don.

The hospital had served the surrounding community for 125 years, mostly providing emergency services and minor surgical procedures, such as tonsillectomies or colonoscopies. If major cardiac surgery was needed or a major medical trauma occurred, people would be either airlifted by helicopter or rushed by a racing ambulance from the speeding E.M.T. Company to the larger town of Bloomington.

Don and the Revealer were about 10 minutes away from the hospital and he still had not spoken a word. Finally, Don, with one hand on the wheel, turned to the Revealer and asked, "Did you cause all of that?"

The Revealer knew precisely what Don was asking, but wanted him to verbalize it. "Cause all of what?"

Don chuckled because he understood what the Revealer wanted him to do. "You know. There was a peace that just, sort of, descended upon the room. I saw You walking around and putting your hands on the shoulders of the ministers."

"How would I fill the room with peace?" the Revealer replied.

"You are God," Don laughed. "You are peace. You bring peace."

The Revealer gazed out the passenger window and quietly said, "Yes, but how We wish that people would receive more."

He turned back toward Don. "Don, the peace of the Father is here for all people, but unfortunately, they fall for all the lies of the evil one. He convinces them that if they have more money or a faster car or a better husband or wife," the Revealer paused, "or bigger churches, they would have peace."

Not wanting to appear materialistic, Don remarked, "That's true, but sometimes people have needs and feel better once they receive them."

The Revealer's eyes opened wider. "The greatest need for humanity is to know the Father. The created will only be fulfilled when they know and have a relationship with the Creator."

Slowly shaking his head, Don acquiesced. "You are right. I didn't mean we should try to replace a connection with the Father with those other things. I guess that is what peace is."

"Now you're getting it," the Revealer said. "Yes, We offer and bring peace, but people have to be willing to receive it. Too many times people are relying upon themselves to capture that elusive peace when We are willing to provide it. With the ministers, they were ready to receive that peace."

"Yes, we all definitely felt it," Don thought. "But why don't You let everyone see You like I can and maybe people would want more peace?"

"We tried that; the Son was seen but rejected. The Son was visible, but people pushed Him away, even accusing Him of being the enemy."

Don slowly lowered his head as if he were the collective representative of shame. "I know. I guess we people don't always know what is good for us."

A large grin spread across the Revealer's face. "Don, that is probably the wisest thing I've heard you say."

As the stoplight on Poplar Avenue turned green, Don steered the car to the right and they entered the asphalt parking lot of the hospital. When they exited the car, Don started a tutorial.

"The hospital was established by the Williams family years ago because they wanted to provide care for their aging parents. Both parents are now deceased and many wanted to name the hospital after them, but the family held firmly to a condition that it be called the Memorial Hospital for all who have passed away. None of the Williamses is still in this area, but their legacy lives on."

"Yes, the matriarch, Marilyn, was a wonderful Godly woman and was missed terribly by her family when she left this side of eternity," the Revealer said.

"Of course, He knew how the hospital started, you dummy," Don thought.

"Don't be so hard on yourself."

They pulled into one of the two parking spots designated for clergy. One of the signs leaned slightly to the left and the "y" on the other one had been smudged by the ravages of weather. It read "clerg only." The ministers teased each other often by referring to those new to their churches and still enjoying their honeymoon phase as "clerg."

Don and the Revealer exited the car and strolled through the entry of the hospital as the glass automatic doors parted for them. The first person they encountered was an older security guard named Ralph. He was a retired deputy sheriff whose face was overwhelmed by a thick, bushy gray mustache. He was friendly, but sometimes forgot that he wasn't a deputy anymore. As a law enforcement officer, he had kept in good physical shape, but, since he retired, he had let himself go.

"Preacher!" Ralph belted out, as he perched on a stool just inside the opening.

"Hi, Ralph, how are you? Have you had any trouble lately?" Don liked to ask Ralph about his day because Ralph would launch into a security briefing, and the stories seemed to get more outlandish each time he saw him.

Ralph started to smile, which caused his mustache to expand even more. "You won't believe this, but you know the Mider brothers? They came here drunk because one of the fools fell out of a tree stand and about broke his dang neck."

Don had heard the story many times; the event had taken place several years ago, but he never interrupted because Ralph enjoyed telling the story. And, as usual, there were new twists. Don appreciated Ralph's imagination.

"Do you know why he keeps telling you the same story?" the Revealer asked Don.

"I'm sure that it makes him feel as if he is important and still has a purpose," Don replied.

"Exactly. You are hearing his heart, and that is why you are willing to hear it over and over again. When we're willing to get to know the hearts of others, we extend much grace to them."

Ralph reached the middle of the story, but added a different twist this time. "Then, I had to grab the brothers with each hand and kick the other one until he calmed down."

The addition of physical force was novel for the story, and Don wanted to hear how this current iteration would end. "What happened then?"

Ralph demonstrated the motions of holding one brother in each arm and only lifted his foot a couple of inches from the ground, simulating his karate skills. "I told them that we weren't going to have any shenanigans in this hospital as long as I'm the security here. And they started behaving."

With admiration in his voice, Don said, "Ralph, I'm sure glad that you're on duty." He grabbed one of Ralph's thick, chubby hands. "But be careful with those two lethal weapons you have!"

Ralph shook his head up and down. "And don't forget my dangerous leg kick, either." He once again attempted to exhibit a tae kwon do kick, but lifted it only a couple of inches off the floor.

"Take care, Ralph," Don smiled and said. "I'll see you after my visits, unless you're taking care of an emergency."

"You can count on me." Ralph waved his pudgy hand in a see-you-later gesture.

"You were very kind." the Revealer said to Don as they moved on.

Don and the Revealer started toward the front desk, which was an oval-shaped island in the middle of the hallway. Off to the left was a waiting room for family members with a loved one going through a surgical procedure. The room was filled with brown, overstuffed chairs and a 32-inch flat screen TV, which blared only dramatic soap operas or even more dramatic cable news.

Tucked into the far-right corner was a tiny room where surgeons consulted with family members after an operation was completed. Boxes of Kleenex tissues were placed throughout the room, as sometimes heartbreaking news was shared. Typically, the surgeons did not stay long, as other patients were prepped and waited for their services.

To the right of the front desk was a small café, with four vending machines dispensing soda pop and stale candy bars. A three-foot counter prominently displayed a plastic container of chocolate cookies. The hours of the café varied, depending on whether a volunteer showed up to tend it.

Seated in a swivel chair behind the front desk was an older woman captivated by a crossword puzzle and oblivious to her surroundings. "Excuse me," Don politely said.

"Yes, may I help you?" she responded, looking up quickly from her little booklet. Don noticed she was new. He had not met her before.

"Yes, I'm Pastor Don from Huron and am here to visit a few people. I don't believe we've met before."

Wrapped in her pink volunteer coat, she extended her hand while still seated and said, "I'm Florence. Nice to meet ya."

Don smiled. "Likewise. I'm here to visit a few people. Would you please tell me their room numbers?" He pulled out a small, crinkled Post-it Note with their names written on it.

"I'd be glad to, honey," she said, putting her booklet aside.

"Honey?" Don thought.

With humor dripping in his voice, the Revealer remarked, "Yes, honey. She could have called you sweetie."

Don grimaced at the Revealer then turned back to Florence. "The names of the people I'm here to visit are Teresa Rogers, Linda Coleman and Max Taylor."

"Thank you, sweetie. It may take me a minute to look them up." She took a second to peer at the keyboard of the computer in front of her.

Don patiently waited and after a few moments of hunting and pecking at the keys, Florence squealed with glee. "I found one, Teresa Rogers." She started to frantically look around. "Now, where is that pad of paper?"

Don leaned over the counter, almost knocking down the "Quiet please" sign and pointed to the pad just to the right of her elbow. Florence giggled. "There it is! Now, what was that name again?"

"Teresa Rogers."

"OK. She's in room 253, and I'll write that down for you because I know that I can never remember anything anyone tells me. Just the other day, I forgot to pick up milk from the market and then I had to go home and make macaroni and cheese, but, you know, it's not any good if you don't put milk in it and it has to be whole milk."

"Thanks for telling me that, but what about the other names?" Don smiled once again.

With an annoying gurgling of a chuckle, she said, "Oh, I told you I forget everything! What were their names again?"

Growing a little impatient, Don slowly repeated, "Linda Coleman and Max Taylor."

"Just one at a time, honey!"

Don shifted his weight, realizing that he was still leaning on the counter after helping Florence find her writing pad. He found himself becoming frustrated with Florence, as the usual volunteer often knew the room numbers of the people Don was visiting before he even asked.

"What's going on?" the Revealer asked Don. "Just a minute ago, you were very patient with Ralph, but now you're allowing yourself to be anxious because Florence isn't as quick as you want her to be."

Don thought back. "I know, but they should have people up front who know what they are doing."

"So, you always know how to do everything when you first start?"

"No, of course not. I need to be more patient."

The Revealer nodded His head.

Florence finally found the room numbers of the other two patients. "Here you go, sweetie." She handed him her findings on the pad of paper with the name of the hospital printed on top.

"Florence, I just want to say thank you very much," Don said, genuinely. "You're doing a good job."

"Oh, honey, that just made my day," she continued, blushing. "Do you know that I had another man yell at me the other day? He didn't think I was doing a good job."

Don waved good-bye. "I'm sure that I'll see you a lot. I'm here once a week."

"Bye, honey."

"Much better," the Revealer said.

"I know. It's about getting to hear their hearts."

Don punched the illuminated button of the elevator to go up. Don thought to himself, "What happens if the elevators are so crowded that the Revealer can't get in?"

"People have been trying to push Us out for years, but it still hasn't worked," The Revealer reminded Don.

Don grinned as the elevator reached the first floor and the doors swished open. A doctor and two nurses quickly exited, along with a family whose daughter had just had a baby. They were carrying helium-filled balloons and oversized cards with "Congratulations" colorfully announcing the birth. Don and the Revealer stepped into the box-like elevator and three other people crowded in as well.

"Floor two, please," one of the fellow elevator passengers called out.

"Floor four for me," another requested.

When the elevator came to a bouncing halt on the second floor, Don excused himself to the woman who was standing squarely in front of the door. He and the Revealer exited and walked through the east hallway, looking for room 253 to find Teresa.

Teresa was an older woman who had attended the Huron church all her life. Although she was short in stature, only 5-feet-2, she stood 8 feet tall spiritually. Teresa had been brought to the church when she was ten days old by her mother, Bonnie. When Teresa was born, Eugene, her father, did not go to church, but he never gave Bonnie a hard time as she packed baby Teresa in her padded carrier and headed out to services every Sunday morning.

Eugene was a hard-drinking man who often retreated into a liquid world, wanting to escape the real one. Bonnie was a sweet woman who worked with the children of the church as much as she could and often found herself kneeling at the small wooden altar in the front of the church with salty tears running down her cheeks.

Bonnie prayed and prayed and prayed for her husband, but it seemed futile and useless. The more she prayed, the more beer cans she found in the trash can. She almost gave up and resigned herself to the fact that her life would never be happy. It looked as if this was her fate, until a tragedy occurred. A young coworker at the factory where Eugene worked, Cooper Johnson, was killed in an automobile accident.

Cooper was driving home from a bar where he and Eugene stopped after working the day shift. The last time Eugene saw the young man he stumbled out the door of the Red Dog Tavern with car keys in his hand. Later that evening, Eugene heard that Cooper had crossed the yellow line in his drunken stupor and collided head-on with an oncoming car.

A young girl in the back seat of the car had unbuckled her seatbelt to pick up a Barbie doll she had dropped. She never knew what hit them. The impact flung her between her parents, who were safely strapped into their seats, through the front windshield. She died instantly, as did Cooper.

Eugene had felt ashamed, as if it was his fault that Cooper and the little girl died. He had a daughter not much younger than the little girl who was killed, and his heart broke when he thought about that night. Eugene sank into a deep depression, fueled by more and more beer.

One evening, 4-year-old Teresa had snuggled up to her father and told him, "I hope that nothing bad ever happens to you because I would really miss you. I'm sure that little girl misses her mom and dad, too." Piercing words from the purity of a child's heart punctured the steel walls surrounding Eugene's soul.

That night, he promised to stop drinking and never looked back. The next Sunday morning, as Bonnie was dressing Teresa in a little pink dress, she was surprised when she saw her husband walk into the room and ask where his tie was. Eugene only owned one tie, an old-fashioned pinstriped one that he had worn for their wedding.

Bonnie stuttered, "It's in the closet . . ." Searching for words, she asked, "Why do you need your tie?"

"I'm going to church with you and Teresa. I need to get saved." With those words, Eugene went to church that Sunday morning and was saved. A few years later, he had admitted he missed the taste of a cold beer after a humid day, but it wasn't worth hurting himself or his family over a few ounces of barley and hops.

In the hospital hallway, Don lightly knocked on the door of room 253. He poked his head inside. "Teresa, are you here?"

He was greeted by a resounding, "You know that I am, Pastor Don. You get in here and pray for me."

Don and the Revealer walked into the small, two-bed room, where one wall was covered with whiteboards with the nurse's information scrawled all over. The other bed was empty. Teresa's bed looked as if it swallowed up her small frame.

She reached out her tiny, bony hand and tightly grabbed hold of her pastor's. "I'm so glad to see you because after we pray for me, we got to pray for all these other people. They really need our prayers."

The Revealer spoke to Don. "In the midst of her pain, she wants to pray for others."

Teresa had been diagnosed with stage-four pancreatic cancer four months earlier. Between her brutal chemotherapy treatments, she tried to spend time at the church when she felt up to it. Other times, the frailty of her flesh would fail her and she just didn't have enough energy. In the last month, she had to be admitted to the hospital twice; the invading cancer seemed to be overwhelming her.

Don tenderly wrapped both of his hands around her petite ones. "Teresa, we love you."

She painfully propped herself up on her elevated bed and squeezed Don's hands with all her might, which was not much. "Oh, Pastor, I love you and everybody, too."

Don noticed that, as she was shifting higher in the bed, pain shot through her body, but she continued smiling. "And, Pastor, you are going to have to forgive me because I didn't do my hair today."

All of her hair had fallen out last month and she teased everyone that she was upset because they visited her without her doing her hair. Without her once-full, wavy brown hair, Teresa looked like a shell of herself, but when she smiled, it was the only thing that he noticed.

"Don, here is a woman who knows the Son and the Father and spends a lot of time with Me," the Revealer said.

Tears welled up in Don's eyes because he knew that it wouldn't be very long before he was looking down into a small wooden casket holding Teresa. She noticed this and playfully smacked his hand with her free hand. "Don't you be crying for little old me. Once I leave this shell, I'm going to be with Jesus!"

Don reverently nodded in agreement. "Teresa, if anyone is going to get into heaven, it will be you."

"You are absolutely right about that," the Revealer concurred.

"Pastor, there are other people for you to visit here. You can't spend all day with me. You have to let other people know about Jesus."

"Yes, ma'am, but before I go, can I pray for you?"

"Yes, but let's not forget about all the others who need prayers, too," she insisted.

"Father, thank you for Teresa. We do ask for you to heal her and that she be surrounded by your presence. And we also pray for all people who need Your healing. In Jesus' name, amen."

"Pastor, thank you, and remember when I die, I want the song 'I'll Fly Away' to be sung as loud as people can."

"Teresa, we won't forget that."

As Don was leaving the room, he turned and glanced once more at this spiritual giant, who he knew would not be on this earth much longer. His thoughts were broken when the Revealer said, "It will not be that much longer, but, trust Me, she will receive a great reward for her faithfulness."

Don and the Revealer walked through the south hallway, looking for room 226, where Linda was a patient. If Teresa was a model of faith, Linda was a model mess. Rarely did anything positive pass through her lips. If there was anything negative that could be found, she was the one to point it out. In many meetings, Don had to bite his tongue as she spit venom toward anyone who was near.

"She needs you to minister to her, too," the Revealer said.

"I know, but it's hard. She's mean."

"I know, but you still have to love her."

By this time, Don and the Revealer were standing next to her room and Don shot a look toward the Revealer, almost begging Him not to have to go in there. But when Don saw the Revealer's face, he took a deep breath, knocked on the door, and hoped that she was asleep.

Of course, she was wide awake and not happy about being in the hospital. She had slipped and fallen, fracturing her right leg. She would only be in the hospital for a couple of days, but it would feel like a tormented eternity for all who would come to see her. As she saw Don, she snipped, "It's about time that you come to visit me."

Don feigned a pastoral smile. "Hi, Linda. Yes, I've come to pray with you. How are you feeling?"

"How does it look like I'm feeling?" she retorted. "I'm in the hospital and my leg is broken and no one will help me when I get back home."

A worker from dietary services came in to collect the plastic food tray from Linda's lunch. She whipped her head in his direction. "That food was terrible! It tasted like rubber and was cold. Dinner had better not be that bad."

"Yes, ma'am," answered the young man, who was wearing a hair net. He made a hasty retreat.

"And another thing," Linda said, on a roll, "the nurses here are terrible. They don't care how you feel. They never help. All they do is bark at me."

Don knew that once Linda launched into a negative tirade, nothing and no one was safe. Don looked at the Revealer as if pleading with Him to help in some way.

"How much do you know about Linda, Don?" the Revealer inquired.

"I know she's one of the meanest people I've ever met and that when she's mad, she's mad at everybody."

"But why is she so upset? What has happened to make her act this way?" the Revealer pressed.

Don paused. "I guess she has had a tough life. It's hard to know how she's been hurt because she lashes out at everything. I know, I know. You want me to hear her heart."

Linda's tongue was wagging faster and faster. "And these doctors are quacks. They don't know anything. I think they're trying to kill me."

Don took a deep breath and extended his hand to Linda, not knowing whether she would reciprocate or not. As she reached out and grabbed his hand, Don spoke slowly. "Linda, I'm sorry that you are hurting and that things are not going well now."

The look of shock was evident in her blue eyes. "Yes, Pastor, it's been terrible. I've been all by myself since my divorce and . . ." her voice trailed off.

Don could not remember how long ago her divorce occurred; it had happened many years ago, long before Don had even heard about the small town of Huron. One day, her husband realized that he had had enough and decided that he needed to get away from her.

Don turned his head toward the Revealer. "That's it. She's so afraid to be hurt by people and have them leave that she strikes first, so she hurts them before they can hurt her."

"Yes. Very sad situation, isn't it?" the Revealer said.

Don continued to look at the Revealer. "But what can you do about someone like this? If you love them, they're still going to be mean."

The Revealer spoke in a manner that felt as if he were shaking Don's soul. "Even though the Son knew He would be rejected, He still loved."

"Love . . . the only force that can never be conquered," Don thought. "Armies have sought to overcome nations, rulers have tried to sustain their political power, but the only thing that survives is love."

"Now you're getting it. So, how can you minister to Linda?"

"I guess I have to love her," Don responded.

"No guess about it," the Revealer said.

"Linda, I want you to know that I love you. I know there have been times when you felt like I've not been the best pastor, and I'm sorry that I've made you feel like that. But I do want you to know that I love you."

Flabbergasted, Linda looked at Don and stammered, "You're not the only one. Every pastor hasn't been nice to me."

Don didn't hesitate. "Linda, if you will help me, I will do my best to help you and be a good pastor for you. Now, can we pray?"

They bowed their heads. Don prayed a sweet prayer for her and slowly leaned forward to offer her a hug. She grabbed hold of him and Don felt a moistness on his shoulder from Linda's tears.

As Don and the Revealer left the room, Linda called out, "I hope to see you again, but you probably won't be back soon." It was another dig, but Pastor Don smiled sympathetically. "I'll do my best."

The Revealer looked amused. "Whoever told you that ministry would be easy?"

Don wanted to fire back something clever, but he knew that the Revealer would know he was being sarcastic.

They made their way back to the elevators and Don told the Revealer, "We'll go up one more floor to the third floor and see Max. Then we can leave. Wait a minute. . . . You know this already."

The Revealer smiled. "Don, the Father and I are used to people telling us how they think things are going to go."

Don stared at the numbers above the elevators and wanted to laugh. "I imagine people often tell You how to do Your job."

The Revealer joined Don in his upward gaze. "You have no idea."

The elevator's "ding" announced they had reached the third floor. Don softly tapped on door 312. Max stirred a little and asked, "Who is it?"

"Max, it's Pastor Don from the Huron Church. Can I come in and pray for you?"

There was a hesitation that seemed to last a long time, but finally Max said, "Sure, come on in." Max did not attend the church, but his Aunt Patty did. She asked Don if he could stop in to see Max when he was at the hospital. Max had just had his gallbladder removed and while usually patients were released the same day, Max had to stay due to unforeseen complications.

"Max, your Aunt Patty asked me to stop by to see you. How are you feeling?"

Max started with a slow drawl. He had not spent too much time talking to preachers. "I'm OK, but they say there is an infection. I might be able to go home in a couple of days."

Don stepped closer to the right side of the bed, away from the sterile tubes of antibiotics running into Max's arm. "Max, I'm a fairly new pastor at the church. Have you ever come to the church?"

Max looked quizzically at Don. "I guess I have been there for a couple of funerals, but church just isn't my thing."

"Let me tell you a secret," Don laughed, "sometimes church is not my thing, but God always is."

Max seemed to take that in. "I guess you're right." He then became quiet. "Do you think that God would take me in?"

"Max, I know that He will always take you in," Don said, his face lighting up.

"Well then maybe, one day, I will come see you."

Don glanced at the Revealer. "Well it's not come to see me, but it's come to see God."

Max tilted his head. "I guess you're right. Will you pray for me?"

"Absolutely." As Don prayed, the Revealer allowed him to see Max's heart. Max was not a bad man. He was a hard worker who put in long hours providing for his family. He loved them and was a good neighbor, but just never got around to thinking much about God.

"Today, you have planted a seed about the Father and it will grow one day," the Revealer said, commending Don.

Don was stunned. "You know what will happen in Max's future?"

"We know all things," the Revealer replied.

After riding down on the elevator, Don and the Revealer walked toward the hospital entryway. Along their path, Don waved at Florence. "Have a great day, Florence!"

She waved back. "You too, sweetie!"

They passed the still-seated Ralph, who appeared as if he was catching a quick catnap. "Ralph, hold down the fort while I'm gone," Don teased.

"Don't worry, preacher. I'm on the job," Ralph replied with pride.

FIVE

Back in the car, Don pulled the seat belt from its shoulder-high anchor and clicked it into place. While he did this, he looked at the Revealer and was about to say, "Please, put your seatbelt on." But then he remembered their conversation last night and chose not to say anything. From the peripheral vision of his right eye, Don thought he saw a faint grin on the Revealer's face.

Don eased slowly out of the parking lot and drove west on Poplar Avenue. Their next destination was the nursing home in Bedford. It was originally named the Donnica Memorial Nursing Center because when the matriarch of the Donnica family died, she left a substantial amount of money on the condition that it be used in some way for the care of senior citizens. Lilly Donnica never believed her family cared enough for her or her husband as they drifted into their golden years, so this was a jab at them for their inattentiveness and also a way to help other older people.

After a new administrator from the West Coast was hired, she immediately renamed it the Bedford Health and Rehabilitation Center. As she presented this change to the staff, she emphasized they were moving into the next century in a progressive way. Even though the facility was renamed and the letterhead changed, the townspeople never called it the Bedford Health and Whatever Center. It was always Donnica Memorial to them.

The BHRC, as a few of the younger staff facetiously called it, stretched out in a star pattern, with a main hub and five extended wings. Each wing was named after a president. The first one to the left of the entrance to the hub was the Washington, then Jefferson, Lincoln, Roosevelt and Reagan. There were 10 rooms in each wing. In the hallways outside the doors, the nurses pushed their plastic carts with drawers filled with pills, medical charts in binder notebooks, and medical supplies.

The hub was the center of frantic activity; many events took place there. Near the entrance was the television room, with a 60-inch flat screen television, that generally played classic movies or the occasional Lawrence

48

Welk rerun. Visitors navigating through this area moved around several residents, either intently concentrating on the television or sadly staring off into space. Then came the large, round nurse's station, which was filled with computers and, usually, a few nurses and aides catching each other up about their weekend escapades.

To one standing at the desk, the outstretched presidential wings were visible. Directly behind the desk was a large room where residents spent time in physical therapy. There were a couple of stationary exercise bikes and a wall lined with very low-weighted, multi-colored dumbbells.

To the right of the PT room was the cafeteria and event area. When it was the cafeteria, residents could either use their walkers or canes, if they needed them, to walk in and sit around the four-person tables. When the large room was not being used as a dining hall, there were activities, including bingo, newspaper reading, and discussions about historical events, to keep the residents busy. This also was the area where incoming guests could play old-time hymns on the wooden upright piano or a guitar player could entertain.

Don always thought that Donnica Memorial, well, Bedford Health and Rehabilitation Center, was not a bad place, but he almost always felt bad after spending time there. As Don and the Revealer passed through the television room, one of the residents reached out a frail, bony hand and Don gently clasped hold of it. Don smiled at the tiny, older woman, who wore a thick gray sweater, even though it felt like it was 80 degrees. She continued to hang on to Don's hand and he had to use his other hand to gingerly remove her tight grip.

The Revealer spoke to Don. "She just didn't want to let go of you. Why do you have a hard time coming here?"

Don glanced at another resident, who did not seem to be lucid, slumped over in his steel, padded wheelchair. He, in a younger time of his life, was tall and muscular and labored many hours as a construction worker, but now time had beaten him down to a shriveled shadow of himself.

"It's just sad," Don thought. "All these people here used to be vibrant and alive, but now it seems as if they are just existing, waiting to die."

The Revealer placed His hand on Don's shoulder to assure him. Don appreciated the gesture and felt a small boost of compassion run through his veins. It was almost as if Don picked himself up and said to the Revealer, "We have a couple of people here. Let's go visit them."

When Don and the Revealer arrived at the desk, which was covered with scattered paperwork and resident chartbooks, Don checked in with one of the nurses. She was enjoying a slice of a pepperoni pizza that had been delivered by a mom-and-pop Italian place down the street. Don said to the nurse as she chomped on another bite, "Hi, I'm Pastor Don and I'm here to visit a couple of my people. Have a nice day."

The nurse smiled between bites of pizza and mumbled with her mouth full, "Have a good day, too."

First, Don visited Charlotte Ditkins, who lived in Room 4 on the Jefferson wing. Charlotte was a sweet woman who once had been extremely active in the church. If there was an event that involved food, Charlotte would provide almost half of it. And Don had been told her pecan pie was to die for. If there was a financial need in the church, Charlotte quietly pulled the former pastors aside and made sure the need was met.

She was married to Henry Ditkins, whose personality was a sharp contrast to that of his kind and generous wife. He was described as a curmudgeon and unpleasant to be around. Don had been told how roughly Henry had treated former pastors, but that had not been his experience. Charlotte entered the nursing home a year before Don became pastor, and Henry visited her every day and spent at least six hours a day with her.

Don admired that about Henry and came to spend time with him as much as he did to visit Charlotte. Charlotte had once been a bundle of energy, constantly moving, cleaning or helping someone else. Then, the cruelty of dementia set in and Charlotte was now a confused, nonverbal shell. Henry sat next to her and tried to hold her hand, even though she didn't recognize her husband of 54 years.

"How's it going, Henry?" Don cheerfully greeted the short, stocky Henry.

"Hi, Pastor Don. It's good to see you. Honey, Charlotte, Pastor Don has come to see you," Henry carefully enunciated every word because Charlotte, who had once been as patient as Job, now snapped at those who spoke too quickly to her and turned her back and looked away.

"Hi, Charlotte. I've come to visit and I see that Henry is with you," Don said as he reached out and patted her shoulder.

"Who are you and why are you here?" Charlotte asked and turned to Henry. "And who are you?"

Tears always welled up in the corners of Henry's eyes when Charlotte frequently posed this hurtful question to him, but he always responded the same way, hoping one day his answer would sink in. "I'm your husband. Over 50 years ago, I saw the most beautiful girl in the world and married her, and now I'm looking at her."

Charlotte's response to his tender answer was to snap back at him. "Well, go and find that girl because she's not here."

"Yes, she is," Henry replied. "I'm not sure where, but I know she's here."

This exchange occurred often when Don visited with them and every time, he steeled himself for the sharp pain he felt from her words. Charlotte peered in the direction of the Revealer.

Don's eyebrows raised in disbelief and he thought, "Can she see You?"

"Of course. She is seeing me right now," said the Revealer.

"I thought that only children could see You," Don said.

"That's true, but there are times when the minds of older people become childlike."

"Hello, sir," Charlotte greeted the Revealer. He smiled at her and leaned forward and embraced her.

Henry's face scrunched up. "You know, Pastor, every now and then she talks to someone or something that is not there."

Don placed his hand on Henry's shoulder. "We don't know, but maybe there is someone there."

Henry, who had once been a mean, unpleasant, and gruff man, teased his pastor. "Please, Pastor Don, don't you lose your mind, too!"

Don laughed. "Don't worry. That happened during seminary."

At the end of every visit, Don would pray with Charlotte and Henry and always conclude with the Lord's Prayer. The first time that he followed this liturgy, he and Henry were instantly stunned. As they recited the Lord's Prayer, Charlotte started saying it with them.

Don was amazed and couldn't believe it the first time it happened. He had stopped at the huge, circular desk on his way out and recounted the event to a nurse. "You're not going to believe this, but I was finishing a prayer with Charlotte and started saying the Lord's Prayer, and she said it with me."

The nurse pleasantly assured him, "Many things are deeply engraved into the minds of the residents and that's why they can remember a childhood event that happened 70 years ago, but can't remember what they ate for breakfast. It's normal."

Don felt relieved, but still stunned. Today, after Don's prayer, he and Henry again began, "Our Father, which art in Heaven . . ."

Charlotte joined in reverently. "Hallowed be Thy name."

Don, Henry, and Charlotte finished the remainder of the prayer. "Thy Kingdom come. Thy will be done on earth as it is in heaven. Give us this day our daily bread, and forgive us our trespasses, as we forgive those who trespass against us, and lead us not into temptation, but deliver us from evil. For thine is the kingdom, and the power, and the glory, forever and ever. Amen."

It was a holy moment when Charlotte was herself again, but it didn't last long. Once Charlotte opened her eyes, she said, "Who are you men in my room?"

Henry had to turn away so that she would not see the tears in his eyes, and Don said, "We'll see you later, Charlotte. We love you. Henry, we love you, too."

After wiping his eyes with a white handkerchief, Henry stood and embraced Don. "We love you, too, Pastor Don. Thank you for letting me have my Charlotte, if only for a brief prayer."

Don smiled and quickly excused himself before his own tears started flowing. As Don passed left, he glanced back and saw the Revealer give Charlotte one more hug.

As they walked together toward the center hub, they veered toward the Roosevelt wing. The Revealer told Don, "You don't get it now, but one day you will."

"I hope you're right," Don wistfully said.

Don felt good about the visit because, even though Charlotte was trapped in the clutches of dementia, she was not mean, and it was good to see Henry. Next, they visited Sabrina Jennings. She was a rotund woman, big in stature, but, more, a giant of rudeness.

Sabrina's great-grandparents had been among the first members of the Huron church, a fact Sabrina didn't let anyone forget. Nothing was right and no one escaped the lashings from her vicious tongue. Former pastors still cringed when they remembered dealing with her. It was as if lions had devoured them.

Since Don had arrived at the church, her terror was not felt as much as it previously had been because she had become a resident in the nursing home three years earlier. Don knocked on the door. "Hello, it's Pastor Don. May I come in for a visit?"

"Who is it?" a shrill voice answered.

"It's Pastor Don," he said patiently.

"Yes, come in. It's about time! You haven't been here forever," she berated him. "You know the other pastors would come and see me every week."

Don's mind reeled because he had met a few of the former pastors and none of them smiled when her name was mentioned. "Sabrina, I come when I can so that I can pray with you."

"You should be here every week; you don't do much. All you have to do is stand up on Sunday and tell everyone else how to live." Then, under her breath, she said, "Most of you preachers aren't living any better than me anyways."

Every fiber of Don's being wanted to lay out his calendar before the crusty crab and show her his schedule, but he refrained. She was on a rampage. "And another thing, no one from the church is coming to see me. They don't care. All they care about is themselves or their grandkids."

Don thought two things: First, when someone says, "and another thing," that's not a good thing and, second, why would anyone want to come and be criticized?

For a second, Don forgot the Revealer stood next to him. "Are you ready now?" asked the Revealer.

Don wanted to close his eyes, like a child knowing a disciplinary action was coming, "I guess so."

"Look around," the Revealer said. "What do you see?"

Don obeyed his instructions, but did not understand why he was surveying the room. "OK, I've done that."

"What do you see?" the Revealer pressed.

Don started to concentrate. Was he missing something? What was he supposed to be seeing? There were only a couple of older pictures hanging on a brown, aged corkboard, which was slightly bent and had the right corner broken off. One picture was of Sabrina and two sisters, who had died at a young age when a drunken driver plowed into their vehicle. In the photo, they were all dressed in frilly dresses and had pigtails and smiles as big as the ocean. You could tell that the trio definitely had at one time been mischievous.

The other picture was of a young Sabrina and her husband, who had become an alcoholic and emotionally and physically abused her. There were no crayon-colored pictures from grandkids. There were no certificates of accomplishment displayed. Just two small, antiquated pictures from bygone days.

"There is nothing here," Don muttered, sadly.

"What do you see in the pictures?"

"Her sisters. They loved each other and probably had a lot of fun. Look at those mischievous grins. I'm sure they gave Sabrina's mother a hard time."

The Revealer said in a hushed tone, "Her mother died right after she was born. Her father raised the three girls by himself. After her sisters died, he couldn't handle it so he committed suicide. Sabrina was the first one to find him."

Don didn't know how to feel. "What about her husband?"

"She got married because she felt she didn't have a choice. They never had children because he was either too drunk or combative. He had watched his father beat his mother so he continued with the hateful traditions he had been taught."

Don's anger flared. "But why didn't she leave him?"

"That was a different time," the Revealer said. "The world was a different place."

Don's thoughts were abruptly interrupted by Sabrina.

"What's wrong with you? Why are you looking at those pictures? You are supposed to be here encouraging me. You are probably the worst preacher that we have had at the church. Pastor Schotts was always wonderful to me. Why can't you be more like him?"

The thoughts that started to run through Don's head now were censored by the Revealer. "Now remember, look at her heart. What is it filled with?"

"I'd like to know if she has a heart," Don said skeptically. "OK, OK, she definitely has been hurt. There have been many changes in the church and it's not like it was when her great-grandparents were involved. And when we're hurting, we want others to hurt, too. But how can I minister to her if she won't let me?"

Don begged the Revealer for an answer. "Don, you are to do what I and the Father ask you, and if you are not received, We will hold them accountable."

Then almost on cue as Don started feeling sorry for Sabrina, she attacked. "And not only that, but you're not that good of a preacher. Pastor Binder's sermons always were good and they were never as long as yours."

Don felt blindsided and thought, "How does she know how I preach? She's been in the nursing home since I've come to the church."

The Revealer told Don, "Remember, negative people attract other negative people. Someone from the church visited her at some point and shared their misguided perspective."

"That was nice of them," Don said.

"Some people are hurting so much that they feel if they can make others feel bad, that it makes them feel good. Don't ever forget, hurting people hurt people."

Don really tried to see her heart, but when he started to feel compassion for Sabrina, she struck vehemently. Almost as if she could read his thoughts, she mounted a particularly hateful diatribe. "You know all these changes that you have made at church are terrible. Communion once a month. No Sunday night service. Why, you don't even wear a suitcoat on Wednesday night!"

Again, Don's adrenaline kicked in and his emotions spiked. "Wear a suitcoat on Wednesday? No, but I still have to wear a stupid tie!"

The Revealer was grinning.

"Why are you grinning?" Don demanded.

"Look at your heart, Don. Her angry heart has contagiously infected your heart. Now you are angry."

Don hung his head. "You're right, but it's so hard to guard my heart when others are being hateful."

"I know," the Revealer said lovingly.

"Of course, You know. People have been hateful to You and the Father and the Son since the beginning. I'm sorry that I'm one of them and I'm sorry that Sabrina has had such a tough life."

The Revealer beamed. "Now, you're getting it."

Sabrina started again. "And I heard that people are leaving the church because they don't like you . . ."

Don cut her off. "Sabrina, I'm sorry I'm not the pastor that you or others think is best, but I'm doing the best I can. Would you please pray for me to learn to be better?"

Flabbergasted, she opened her eyes wide in shock. "You're supposed to pray for me!"

Don spoke with compassion. "I do pray for you and I am going to continue to do so."

Don paused and launched into a beautiful prayer, in which he blessed her and hoped that peace would fill her heart.

As he exited the room, Sabrina fired one last shot. "I'm sure I probably won't see you for a long time now."

Don waved and smiled. "God bless you, Sabrina."

As they walked back toward the middle hub, the Revealer coached Don. "Some people are never going to let you minister to them. You keep doing the best you can and being obedient to Us and it will all work out."

Don managed a weak smile, hoping what the Revealer said was true. In the middle of the hallway, the Revealer stopped walking, turned to Room 2, and stepped inside. Don didn't know what was happening. Had the Revealer been summoned? Was the Revealer tired of working with Don? And then he found himself almost knocked over by a blur of nurses rushing toward Room 2.

One of them was shouting something about a code and Don was confused. Another one barked back toward the hub to see whether the doctor was still in the facility. Then they disappeared into the room where the Revealer had stepped. Don found himself caught up in the whirlwind, his curiosity took over, and he joined the growing, buzzing mob in room 2.

"Please step aside, sir," a nurse requested.

Don slowly entered the room and saw the nurses examining a male resident who didn't appear to be breathing. One nurse held the resident's blue notebook chart and started speaking in medical terminology, a foreign tongue to most bystanders. "It says DNR, per patient's wishes," the nurse with the chart announced.

Don knew that DNR meant Do Not Resuscitate. If a resident requested a DNR, he or she would not be revived if their body started to shut down. Then it hit Don that the man was either dying or had already passed into eternity. One nurse, visibly shaken, stepped toward the man and placed a stethoscope on his bony chest to see if she could find a heartbeat. After a few seconds, she slowly shook her head side-to-side.

The shoulders of the nurse holding the chart slumped and Don could see a sadness in her eyes. The third nurse in the room turned to leave and said for Don's benefit, "There's nothing we can do. He's gone." Lifting her stethoscope off his chest, the nurse stoically announced, "Call the doctor to pronounce the time of death at 3:45 p.m."

Don's feet became clay and he felt as if he were a statue. He had never seen anyone die before. Sure, he had officiated at almost 20 funerals in his first three years of ministry, but he had never been in the same room when someone took a last breath. Then, it was as if Don came out of fog and he looked around for the Revealer.

As the remaining nurses quietly left, one turned to Don. "Are you family?

Don shook his head. "No, I'm a pastor."

Then Don saw the Revealer. He had been in the room the whole time, even before the nurses rushed in. The Revealer was seated next to the man, but was completely bent over holding him tightly. Don's first reaction was to say something, but no words made sense. Don watched for a while as the Revealer appeared to be tenderly rocking the man back and forth much like a mother with a newborn.

Then the room was bathed in an almost blinding light. Don raised his arms quickly and used his hands to shield his eyes. A sense, or a feeling of something Don couldn't comprehend, came over him. It was the same presence as the night that the Father spoke to him. Don slowly pulled his hands away from his eyes and he saw the room filled with angelic beings, spirit creatures that were beautiful and peaceful and strong. They were emanating with a power that Don had never experienced. An inexpressible joy seemed to flow from their essence.

Don froze, terribly frightened, but he also felt an overwhelming warmth. Then the Revealer slowly rose and, in His arms, He held what appeared to be another spirit being. The Revealer turned and affectionately handed off the spirit He had been holding to one of the angelic beings and then, in an instant, they disappeared through the ceiling of the room.

Don's head reeled and he started rubbing his eyes. "Surely, I did not just see what I thought I saw."

Standing in the room were only two now, Don and the Revealer.

"What, what, what just happened?" were the only words that Don could form in his mind.

"Don, you were given another gift. The Father allowed you to see what happens when one of His children goes home to be with Him."

"So, he died. I mean he passed away. I mean, he's not here with us," Don stuttered.

"You're right. He is no longer with us. He is with the Father and Son in Paradise."

Don didn't know if he should ask this question or not. "But what would have happened if he did not know You and the Son and the Father?"

The Revealer spoke solemnly. "It is the most heartbreaking event of all eternity."

"So, what happens now?" Don's head was swirling.

"His former body is now just a shell, a temporary dwelling place. You humans will dispose of it in some form, but it was never designed to last forever," the Revealer said. "Let's go and talk about this outside because the nurses will come in and have to take care of his body."

Just then, a couple of nurses entered the room. "Thanks for saying a prayer for him, Pastor. Now, please excuse us. We have to take care of him."

Don maybe said, "you're welcome," or maybe he didn't. He was still trying to figure out what he had seen.

As they walked past the nurse's desk, Don turned to the Revealer. "You would have to be a special person to be a nurse, wouldn't you?"

The Revealer looked at them with appreciation. "More than you know."

Outside by the car, Don stopped. "OK, I just want to make sure that I saw what I saw. A man died. You were holding him and then a whole bunch of, what were they angels, they came and took him to heaven?"

"Yes."

"That's how it works? When we die, a welcoming committee comes and then we get taken to Heaven?"

"Something like that," said the Revealer.

"But there was a death. Shouldn't we be sad?" Don tried to untangle all his balled-up feelings.

"You humans think of death as finality, but it's just the beginning," explained the Revealer.

"The beginning? It looked like the end to me."

"That's because people don't understand death. Death is not to be feared. Don, you know the scriptures. Death has been swallowed up in victory. Death has no sting."

Don felt as if he'd been corrected. "Yes, I know the scripture verses about death, but a man died. I mean, he really died."

"In your understanding, he died. Don, death is not an end. When a human dies who has been brought to the Father through the Son, that person is more alive than ever," the Revealer taught.

Don placed his hands on the side of the car and leaned forward. "I know all that, but it's sad when someone dies."

"Yes, it is. People are sad for themselves. They won't be able to spend time with their loved one again. But they shouldn't be sad for the person."

Don had trouble comprehending the event. "What do you mean, we shouldn't be sad for that person? I'm sad for that man and I don't even know his name."

"Joel, Joel Minster." the Revealer said. "That's his name. Do you want to know what the Father called him when he first appeared in heaven?"

"Yes!"

"The Father said, 'Welcome home, son.' He called him son," replied the Revealer.

"And Joel has now been reunited with his mother, father and grandmother, and they are joining with the celestial choirs, celebrating. He is no longer confined to a bed. He has no pain. He is whole."

Don pushed back from the car. "So, do you and the Father and the Son think that we people are dumb because we are so sad when someone dies, I mean, goes to heaven?"

"Oh, no. We understand that people love, and grieving is an expression of love. Mourning is one of the emotions the Father gave you. It's not wrong to grieve and be sad, but hold onto the fact that if your loved one knew the Father, that person is more alive than ever before."

Don grabbed the Revealer's hand. "This is almost more than I can figure out."

The Revealer laughed. "Don, you're going to spend all of eternity learning more and more about the Father. Do you think you'll have Him figured out in a week?"

Don laughed, too.

SIX

Don pulled into the driveway at the parsonage, barely avoiding a small bicycle abandoned on the sloped pavement. "I've told him a million times not to leave his bike there," Don snapped.

"Think of how many times the Father has told His children to do things," the Revealer said.

"You're right. I guess we're all in process, whether we're 4 years old or almost 30," Don said.

Don moved the bike next to the garage and he and the Revealer walked to the front door. "Spend time with your family. You will see Me tomorrow morning at the church," the Revealer said.

"OK, so you're not coming in with me?"

"Don, We're always with you, but you have a lot to process and need to enjoy your kids. They change and grow up quickly."

"Sounds good," Don said, turning to open the front door. As Don twisted the knob and pushed the door open, he was greeted by loud squeals and a raucous chorus of "Daddy's home!"

Thursday evenings were generally quiet around the Stouts' home. Debbie would cook dinner and tonight was tacos, one of their favorite meals. Erin meticulously filled her soft-shelled tortillas, while Nathaniel's looked as if an atomic bomb had dropped on his plate, scattering lettuce, cheese, meat and broken-up shells everywhere.

After dinner, they pulled Candyland and Chutes and Ladders board games from the closet and spread them over the floor of the living room. Bursts of laughter erupted from the children; Don and Debbie cherished these times. When the fun subsided, it was bath time with lots of bubbles.

Debbie accompanied Erin during her bath time, but was reminded that Erin was getting older and able to take care of herself. She was 6 years old, after all. As Erin emerged from the bathroom in a fluffy purple bathrobe with a towel snugly wrapped around her wet hair, Don was amazed at how much she resembled her mother.

Then it was Nathaniel's turn. Sometimes, it was easy and sometimes the bathroom looked like a hurricane had swept through, with every surface soaked with water. There were times that Don initiated the damp playfulness, but he was more reflective tonight. So, Don was thankful when Nathaniel was content to play with his little green army men in a subdued manner.

As Debbie tucked the kids into bed, Don wandered into the living room, plopped down on the floral-print couch, and inhaled deeply. Just last night, he had experienced an incredible encounter with the Living Lord, the Father, and, today, he had spent time with the Revealer. While not much time had passed since Wednesday night, so much had taken place.

Don reflected about the ministers' meeting and how the Revealer walked around the room, placing His hands on each of their shoulders.

"How many times has that happened that I had an instant peace but didn't know why?" Don thought.

Don retraced their steps through the hospital and nursing home. He had learned so much today, but still wasn't able to conceptualize everything that was taking place.

Debbie ran her fingers through her hair as she sat down on the padded couch next to Don. "Did they go down without a fight?"

"They were worn out tonight. They rode their bikes all afternoon."

"Yes, I know. I almost ran over Nathaniel's as we pulled in," Don said with a slight hint of exasperation.

"That boy. You know, he's just like his father," Debbie joked.

"That hurts! Here I am, looking for some compassion and all I get is ridicule," said Don.

"You'll be all right. How was your day?" asked Debbie.

"It was interesting. A lot happened today."

Debbie snuggled in, pulling a multi-colored comforter over herself. "Tell me about it."

Don didn't know where to begin. "First, I had been assigned to share the devotion at the ministers meeting, but I forgot to prepare one."

Debbie lifted her head from Don's shoulder. "That's not like you, honey. You're normally prepared."

"I know, but it worked out perfectly. The Holy Spirit showed up and I think we ministered to each other," Don assured her.

She lowered her head back on his shoulder and her hair tickled his neck. "Then we went to the hospital to visit people," he said.

Curiosity rose in Debbie's voice. "We? Did Pastor Liddle go with you to the hospital?"

Don stammered, "No, uh, what I meant was, God was with me."

"As He is always with us, all the time." Debbie's faith constantly amazed her husband. "Who did you see there?"

"Teresa, Linda, and Max," Don answered.

Debbie wrapped her arms around Don. "Oh, that's nice. How are they? And who is Max?"

"Teresa was sweet, as usual, and Linda was not so sweet, as usual." Don stifled a laugh. "But you know, Linda has had much pain in her life. We need to pray for her. And Max is Patty's nephew who just had an operation, but has an infection, so he may need to stay for a couple of days. Nice guy. He said he might come to church sometime."

"That's nice." Debbie knew Don's Thursday routine so she asked, "How was the nursing home?"

Don lurched forward. "I can't believe I haven't shared this with you!"

"What? Is everything all right?"

Don settled back and pulled Debbie close to him. "Yes. I saw a man die today."

Debbie quickly leaned forward. "Are you OK? Was it sad? Who was it?"

Don was rarely astonished by Debbie's rapid-fire questioning; she seemed to be able to handle many things all at one time. "His name was Joel Minster and he had a wonderful relationship with the Father."

Debbie's eyebrows furrowed. "Did you know him? How did you know he had a good relationship with God?"

"No, I didn't know him, but there was a peace in the room that I can't begin to explain. It was filled with legions of angels." Don's mind relived the scene.

"Wow, it sounds like you've had a full day," she said. With that, they huddled together, holding each other before slowly walking back to their bedroom for a good night's rest.

On Fridays, Don arrived at the church around 7 a.m. to start working on his sermon for Sunday. As he was awakened by the serenade of the alarm clock, he was surprised there was not a knock on his bedroom door like yesterday. He arose, showered, dressed and headed to the kitchen to eat a couple of pieces of toast.

As Don walked down the hallway, he looked around, wondering where the Revealer was. "He told me that He was going to spend the whole week with me," Don thought.

Instantly, the Revealer spoke to Don. "I'm here, just waiting in the car."

Don was puzzled. "So, even when You are not right next to me, You know what is going on?"

"Don, you are never alone," the Revealer said. "You may not always be able to see me, but I'm always with you."

Don finished his buttered toast and rushed through a cup of instant coffee because he didn't want to make the Revealer wait. He gripped the handle of the car door and pulled it open. "I'm sorry to make you wait."

The Revealer's face reflected a deep peace. "Don, don't worry about that. The Father makes all things happen in His time. You people are much more worked up about time than We are."

Don backed out of his driveway, making sure that he didn't plow over any more of Nathaniel's landmines. As they turned into the gravel parking lot of the church, Don thought about their first ride together and smiled. "I started chauffeuring the Revealer around a couple of days ago."

Don took the brass key out of his pocket and unlocked the double glass doors leading into the small square foyer. Straight ahead were three steps, leading to the petite sanctuary. To the left were six steps, leading to the church's basement.

In the basement, there were four rooms adjacent to a larger one, which held three long, white plastic tables used for church dinners and committee meetings. Along the north side of the room, known as the fellowship hall, or the "eatin' place," was an older stove. It had been used for many years, evidenced by the built-up grease from many church dinners.

There was also a light-green Whirlpool refrigerator, which many cherished because it was the grand prize of a raffle for the volunteer fire department of Lawrence County. Eldene had bought only one ticket to support the fire department, and when urged to buy more, she remarked, "If God wants us to have it, it will take only one ticket." She was right and her critics were silenced.

In between the aluminum-handled stove and the treasured refrigerator was about three feet of a light-brown granite countertop. A cheap, low-power black microwave, which barely had enough juice to pop a bag of popcorn, sat next to a Mr. Coffee pot with a well-used carafe. Perched above the countertop were four darkly stained wooden cabinets, where some dishes and pots and pans made their homes.

One of the four rooms of the basement was the pastor's office and the other three were set up as Sunday school rooms, two for children and one for adults under the age of 60. For people over 60 years old, the Sunday school class met in the sanctuary upstairs, so they only had to walk up the three steps once.

Don and the Revealer veered left and descended the steps to his office. As Don opened the door, he cautiously looked around, checking whether it was the same place. He walked around his desk, making sure he didn't hit his knee again, sat down in his Walmart chair, and started rearranging a couple of piles of paperwork to create a clear space to work.

There was one padded folding chair on the other side of Don's desk and the Revealer sat down on it. Don peered at Him. "OK. Would you please give me a sermon?" He was half-joking and half-serious.

The Revealer's countenance was kind. "What lessons have you been learning?"

"Lessons I have been learning?" Don repeated. "I could preach for a year on what I have learned in the last 32 hours."

"Good. What lesson does the Father want you to teach His people?"

Don slipped into deep thought. "I think the biggest lesson that I needed, and still need, is to listen to the hearts of others."

A large smile crossed the Revealer's face. "Yes, and what would be a good scripture passage to examine about listening to the hearts of others?"

Several passages raced through Don's mind, but he kept coming back to one. "The text of Jesus asking the disciples who people said He was, but then probing deeper. He asked them 'Who do you say I am?'"

The Revealer nodded in agreement. "Excellent. What are some of the points we can bring out in the sermon with this text?"

Don was on a roll. "First, what is in our hearts is important to God. Second, God wants us to share what's in our hearts with Him. And, third, we should listen to the hearts of others."

"I think that will preach," agreed the Revealer.

Don stood and strolled over to the bookshelf, which held several thick Biblical commentaries, and plucked a couple of his favorites from their assigned locations. Then he grabbed the hefty, hardcover Strong's Exhaustive Concordance and started forming a tower of knowledge on his desk.

Opening his blue, hardcover Bible, Don studied and searched, spending time learning more and more about the passage he was going to preach about on Sunday. As he fervently worked, the Revealer sat quietly, in full accord with what was happening in Don's heart. Occasionally, Don would raise his eyes to see whether the Revealer approved of what he was compiling. He was encouraged when the Revealer continued nodding his head affirmatively.

Normally, it took Don eight to ten hours to prepare a sermon, a process stretching over a couple of days, but today it seemed to just flow from him quickly. Of course, having the Holy Spirit sitting across from him on the other side of his desk made things a little easier.

After a few hours, Don sat back, placing his hands behind his head and intertwining his fingers. "There. I think it's done."

The Revealer, happy with Don's message, but not wanting him to be overly confident, said, "A sermon is never done. Sometimes, I will lead you another direction, even while you are preaching."

Don's eyes opened wide. "That's what has happened! There have been times when all of a sudden I thought of a scripture verse or a point that I had not thought of before."

"You're welcome," said the Revealer.

"Being able to see you is a greater gift than I will realize on this side of eternity, isn't it?" inquired Don.

"Yes, and never forget, to whom much is given . . ."

Don interjected, "much is required."

The Revealer stood up and said, "Let's go and make those visits."

Don wanted to ask how He knew what his Friday routine was, but then caught himself.

Striding up the steps, Don grabbed hold of the flimsy wooden handrail and noticed that a couple of screws had fallen out. After locking up, Don turned toward the parking lot and noticed Roger Terren in front of his house, working on a lawn mower. Roger lived diagonally from the church, on the south corner, and many years ago had been an active member.

Roger's feelings had been hurt when he was not voted to be on the Board of Trustees. He truly believed that God wanted him to serve in that capacity, but thought that the people must not have listened to Him. There were several other issues that bothered Roger and, instead of sticking around to work through them or overcome them, he decided not attending church was his best option.

Don regularly walked over to Roger's older two-bedroom home and talked with him on his porch. Roger was always polite, but continued to keep a physical distance from the church building and an emotional distance from Don. Don knew many of the details of why Roger didn't attend anymore, but wanted to continue to reach out to him. Don thought, "Maybe someday, he will come around."

Don waved to Roger. "Working hard or hardly working?"

Roger shot his free hand up; his other hand was stuck in the motor of the half-torn-apart lawn mower. "You know that I work hard."

With a friendly tone, Don invited him to church once again. "I'd love to see you this Sunday, Roger."

Roger's face shifted to the lawn mower's motor. "Don't hold your breath, preacher." The words were not meant to be hurtful and Don did not take them as so, but they signified that Roger still was hurt.

Don waved again. "OK, but if holding my breath would get you into the church, you might see me with a blue face and my cheeks pushed out."

Roger started chuckling. "You are a crazy preacher."

As Don and the Revealer settled into their seats in the car, Don turned to his passenger. "His heart is hurt, but how long is he going to hold onto it? All the bad things that happened at that time have been resolved, and most of it happened a long time ago."

The Revealer wisely said, "Many people like to hang on to hurts. They feel that if they forgive and move on, they will be hurt again."

Don was filled with compassion. "Wouldn't that be a lonely life?"

"Yes, it would."

The first home visit was going to be to Faye Bowder, who lived up a steep hill on a pea gravel road, right off State Route 50. Faye had once attended the church regularly and was extremely active in its activities, but had to slow down. She was rebounding from a bout with cancer. She often would laugh and say, "The devil tried to take me out, but God isn't ready for me to come home yet."

The first time Don went to visit Faye, he got terribly lost because the directions read "turn right at the second oak tree and then after a little while, turn left where the Sowders store used to be." Don wasn't quite sure of the difference between an oak or an elm tree and he definitely didn't know where the old mercantile had been located.

Don had finally found it and mapped out a route in his mind that didn't include having to know what type of tree was where. Faye lived in an old, rustic trailer that appeared to be abandoned; the white siding on the front was faded and falling off in small sections. Despite her house appearing as if it should be condemned, Faye was one of the sweetest women who had ever lived.

Don joked to the Revealer, "You should have been with me the first time I looked for her place. I was so turned around, but, somehow, I finally found it."

The Revealer gazed at Don. "You're welcome."

Don shook his head. "I know, I know, You were with me then."

As they pulled into the driveway, they parked next to a pile of wood that had once been stacked, but had toppled over. Faye's only heat was a wood stove and her second cousin's son brought her chopped and quartered wood for fuel. Sometimes, he stacked it. Sometimes, he didn't feel like it.

Stepping out of the car, Don surveyed the scene around Faye's dilapidated trailer, taking in the gorgeous flowers, the grassy knolls and the many sturdy trees. She lived way back in the woods. Faye had an alarm at the end of her makeshift driveway that would alert her when people drove up. Most days it was silent, since Faye didn't have many visitors, but once a month her new, young minister came by.

As Don and the Revealer sauntered toward her sagging wooden steps, which had been beaten down by rain and snow, Faye stood in the doorway, cackling and waving. "Get in here, preacher."

Don loved Faye. She was a tough country woman who had lived a hard life, but was one of the happiest people he had ever met. "Hello, Faye. How are you today?"

Her common response was, "Finer than frog's hair." Don never truly understood whether that was good or bad.

As Don's foot stepped on the last rickety step, Faye grabbed hold of him in a bear hug and squeezed. Faye was a big woman, standing at least 6-feet-3. She was big-boned and strong as an ox, even though she was in her mid-70s.

The hug took Don's breath for a second. "It's good to see you."

Faye backed up, pulling Don into the worn-out, deteriorating trailer and directed him to a nearby red recliner. Every time Don visited with her, she insisted he sit there. "That's where my dear husband always sat, so I want you to sit right there."

As Don made himself comfortable in the oversized recliner, which was not as padded as it had been at one time, Faye rushed over to her miniscule kitchen, which contained a small table and two wooden chairs. "You like your coffee with no cream, right, Pastor?"

"Yes ma'am. You have a good memory."

Faye carried two mismatched cups of steaming coffee to the living room, where she sank into her own recliner. The cast-iron wood stove was in the living room as well, and when Faye fed the logs into it, it generated so much heat it almost made the room uncomfortable. The living room was on the right end of the trailer. Just a couple of feet from it was the kitchen, where Faye prepared the coffee.

There was a small hallway and a bathroom with just enough room for a tiny toilet and a bathtub that seemed to be made for a child. The only bedroom was on the left end of the trailer. Don had once tried to figure out the dimensions of the trailer and decided it couldn't have been longer than 30 or 40 feet and more than 10 feet wide. It didn't seem to be adequate living space for a person.

Faye didn't own much. Her late husband, Dennis, had worked as a mechanic in a garage in Bedford, but never had a 401(k) or any other retirement plan. Faye's Social Security check placed her far below the poverty line. In spite of Faye's poor living conditions and meager possessions, she was one of the most joyful people who Don had ever met.

"Pastor, what have you been doing lately? How is the church doing?" She looked at him over her wire-rimmed glasses. "Is everyone behaving there or do I need to come and put some people over my knee and spank them?"

Don almost spit out his coffee. He thought, "I could give you a couple of names who need to be spanked," but merely responded, "No, Faye, things are well."

Faye started snickering. "Pastor, the other day, I looked out this window and wouldn't you know it, a red squirrel was standing on my porch looking back at me."

Don loved her stories because she found fun in everything. "What happened then?"

Faye continued and started guffawing. "I was going to let him in and give him a TV dinner."

Don laughed so hard he almost spilled his coffee. He pictured a squirrel sitting with her, eating a TV dinner. Being around an enjoyable person like Faye was always fun. Don looked over at the Revealer and saw that He was having an entertaining time, as well.

Faye pushed on the arms of her recliner and slowly struggled to her feet. "Pastor, you have to get going and visit other people. You don't have all day to sit here with an old, broken-down woman talking about squirrels. So, get over here and pray for me."

Faye loved visitors, but when she was ready for them to leave, she was ready. Don walked the few feet back to the kitchen, emptied his coffee cup, and placed it in the sink, "Is there anything I can pray for you today?"

Faye's face broke into a full smile. "Pastor, God is so good to me; I want us to pray for other people."

After each visit with Faye, Don found himself a little happier and more appreciative. With her large, strong hands, Faye grabbed the hands of her pastor. He prayed that God would bless her and help everyone who needed help.

A loud and resounding "amen" echoed from the depths of Faye's soul. "Pastor, I love you and thanks for coming by. I'll see you next month."

"Faye, yes, you will. We love you. Give us a call if you need anything."

"Bless you, bless you, but God and me are doing good," Faye assured Don.

After one last wave, Don started the car and slowly backed away, making sure not to run over any hungry, TV-dinner-eating squirrels. The Revealer spoke softly. "She is a wonderful woman and soon she will be going home with the Father."

This was a fact that Don knew, but didn't want to acknowledge. Faye's health was not good, but she would never admit it because she didn't want anyone to feel bad for her. The Revealer asked Don, "What is in Faye's heart?"

Don snapped from his brief sadness, thinking that Faye would not be here on earth much longer, and replied, "There is a children's song that they sing in children's church: 'I have the joy, joy, joy, joy, down in my heart.' That's what I think is in Faye's heart."

The Revealer agreed. "Anyone who missed the joy of the Lord in her heart would be sadly misguided."

Backtracking through the woods, following Don's improvised directions, he and the Revealer headed to the house of Nanny Bridges. Nanny was another Godly woman who had been a pillar at the church until an unfortunate event. At the age of 34, she had been involved in a horrific car accident that had killed her 14-year-old son, Jerry. It left her paralyzed and confined to a bed.

Nanny was now 87 years old and had been bedridden for 53 years. She had endured 53 years of others feeding her, 53 years of being unable to move, 53 years subjected to the confinement of a hospital bed. Her oldest son, John, refused to let his mother spend her life in a medical facility, so he brought her home, quit his job, and became her full-time caregiver.

If anyone in the world had reasons to be angry with God, it was Nanny Bridges. On that nightmarish night, much of her life had been stolen from her. But instead of becoming a bitter, mean, resentful person, Nanny was one of the sweetest encouragers who ever lived.

Three years ago, when Don drove to meet Nanny for the first time, he struggled with what he should say and how he could encourage a person trapped in a hospital bed and imprisoned in an immovable body. As soon as Don walked into the log cabin where Nanny lived, she had flashed a toothless grin at him. "I'm sorry, Pastor, but my teeth have jumped out of my mouth."

Don hadn't known what to do. Should he look for them? Should he call someone? "I'm sorry. Can I help you find them?"

John had walked into the room from the kitchen. "Mom, you're not scaring this new young preacher with your teeth, are you?"

She beamed from ear to ear. "I wanted to welcome him." Don sighed a breath of relief when he realized he had just been initiated into Nanny's fellowship.

Nanny had the most positive attitude of anyone Don had ever met. She listened to cassette tapes of every service at the church and when Don visited, she told him how good his sermons were and that she could tell how much he studied. Every time Don went to visit Nanny, he thought, "I'm going to minister to her this time, not her to me." But after each visit, he realized how much she had lifted him up instead.

Don and the Revealer stopped at the end of the gravel driveway that led to the log cabin and walked to the front door. As Don rang the doorbell, he was greeted by John with a friendly, "Mom, your dentist is here." Teeth jokes had become a part of their normal ritual after Don's first visit with Nanny.

Nanny's metal, amply padded hospital bed was in the living room, where she could watch TV and listen to the church services on her Sony audio cassette player. As Don and the Revealer entered her living space, Nanny perked up. "Pastor, it's good to see you, but you're not alone."

Don was astonished. "It's good to see you, too, but why do you say I'm not alone?"

Nanny's eyes methodically shifted back and forth, scanning the room. "I feel that someone is with you."

Don hesitantly responded, "God is always with us."

Nanny agreed, "Yes, He is, but His presence is more powerful today than normal. Thank you for coming. You've made my day!"

Don thought to himself, "There she goes again, encouraging me!"

The Revealer walked over to Nanny's bedside and reached out his hand and tenderly placed it upon her head. Nanny closed her eyes and started singing, "Holy Spirit, You are welcome in this place."

John looked at Don quizzically, but Don knew what was going on. Nanny was such a Godly woman; she knew the presence of the Holy Spirit. Don slowly sank into a nearby chair and felt like an observer of someone spending time with God. A peace that could almost be physically touched filled the room.

John sat down, too, but just wasn't sure what was happening. After Nanny sang a few more hymns, her face beamed. "Pastor, thank you so much for coming. You brought the Holy Spirit with you to come see me."

"Nanny, I know that you spend a lot of time with the Holy Spirit," Don's responded.

"Yes, there is a sweet Spirit here with you today."

"Nanny, you are a sweet spirit. Thank you." Don felt his eyes moisten.

"Pastor, would you pray for us? And after you pray, I want to pray for you and your family."

Don and John gathered around Nanny's bed, each holding one of Nanny's hands in theirs. John could not see it, but the Revealer was standing behind them, placing His hands on their shoulders. After Don prayed, Nanny launched into a prayer so gorgeous that Don believed even the angels had to pause to listen to it.

As they were leaving, Don told Nanny, "I will be back to see you. Thank you for being so sweet."

Nanny returned a gaze to him that warmed his heart. "I love you, Pastor."

"We love you, too, Nanny."

Back in the car, Don stared straight ahead. "She did not see You but she knew You were there."

"Nanny spends much time with Us. She is one of our warriors. You feel bad because she is physically weak, but you have no idea how spiritually powerful she is."

As they got on State Route 50 to return to Huron, Don's head was spinning at the interaction between Nanny and the Revealer. He marveled at how close she was to God and his heart desired to be that deep as well.

SEVEN

Slowly, Don pulled into his driveway, still watching for Nathaniel's toys. As he and the Revealer exited the car, the Revealer told Don, "It's Friday night. Go and enjoy your family and I will meet you in the morning when you go to the Bedford Walmart."

Don's looked perplexed. "I won't be going to Walmart tomorrow."

"I'll be in the car waiting for you in the morning," the Revealer said.

"You may be there for a while," Don mumbled.

"Have a good evening with your family," the Revealer said as he walked away.

Don shook his head in bewilderment and turned toward the house, walking up the three steps of his porch. Entering the house, he noticed an eerie stillness. Usually, when he came home, he was greeted with a duo who caused enough commotion to be mistaken for a thundering herd of buffalo. But tonight it was different.

Don took off his maroon jacket, hung it in the hallway closet, and decided he needed to investigate why it was so quiet. "Debbie, Erin, Nathaniel, where is everybody?" Don called out. No answer, so Don beckoned more loudly. "Debbie, Erin, Nathaniel?" Still no answer. "Where can they be?" Don wondered.

As he walked through the house, Don peered into each bedroom and still couldn't find anyone. He thought to himself, "There's no way that they could be in the basement, could they?" He decided to look there.

As he started descending the carpeted steps into the basement, he heard loud squeals of delight. "So, this is where everybody is hiding. Why are you down here?"

"Daddy, Daddy!" chanted Erin and Nathaniel in unison. "Can we keep him, huh, huh?"

Don was puzzled. "Keep who?" he asked and noticed Debbie, Erin and Nathaniel were huddled around a brown cardboard box, gazing at its contents. It dawned on him that there might be an animal in the box and he intently looked at Debbie. "I thought we were going to wait until both kids were in school before we got a pet?"

Debbie smiled and threw her hands up in the air in mock surrender. "Eldene came by to 'dust' our shelves and said she had a stray pup on their ranch that needed a good home."

Don inched his way closer to the box. Inside was a tiny brown-and-tan dachshund puppy, whose eyes seemed to be much too big for his head. His little paws didn't seem to be long enough to carry his elongated body. "Can we keep him; can we keep him?" the kids cried again.

"Who is going to take care of him?" Don asked, but knew he would become the primary caretaker when the novelty of a new pet wore off.

"We will, we will!" Nathaniel and Erin answered gleefully.

"OK. But having a dog is a big deal and we don't even know his name." As those words fell out of Don's mouth, the puppy cast a droopy-eyed stare that melted his heart.

"His name is Stretch because he's very long," Erin boldly announced.

"Stretch it is," agreed Don.

Debbie wrapped her arms around Don and snuggled in. "How was your day, honey? Oh, and, by the way, since Stretch is staying now, I have some things that you have to get at Walmart tomorrow. Is that all right?"

Don flashed back to the words of the Revealer telling him they were going to Walmart tomorrow. "Sure, not a problem."

The rest of the night was filled with giggles as Stretch explored his new home with the Stouts.

As Don strode toward his car in the morning, the Revealer was sitting in the passenger seat. He greeted Don with a friendly "Good morning."

"Good morning to You. You knew all along we were going to go to Walmart, didn't You?" he said, shaking his head.

"How is Stretch?" the Revealer snickered.

Don paused and, once again, shook his head.

As they crossed over the bumpy railroad tracks and left Huron, they turned east toward Bedford. Following winding, hilly State Route 50, Don drifted into deep thought.

"You're wondering whether We know everything." It was not so much of a question, but rather a statement presented by the Revealer to Don.

"Yes, I was. You knew what Debbie was thinking and You even knew what Erin was going to name our new houseguest. How? Do You know everything? Do we decide anything that surprises You?" So many questions were racing at lightspeed through Don's mind.

"Yes, We know. We know all things and are not surprised," the Revealer answered.

Don truly was mystified. "But does that mean that we really don't have a choice in anything because You know what we are going to do?"

"No, Don, people have free will. When the Father created you, He gave you the privilege of choice. If you didn't have the right to choose, then how could you choose to love the Father? We know what you are going to choose, but you solely have made that decision," explained the Revealer.

"This doesn't make any sense to me."

"Many things don't make sense for you as people. Just trust and We will take care of you," assured the Revealer.

"Trust is hard," Don said.

The Revealer's eyes bored into Don's soul. "We know. Father, help his faith."

They arrived in Bedford and swung north onto Main Street. It took traversing up and down four aisles of parking spaces, dodging people pushing overfilled shopping carts, before they were able to find a spot. "Saturday morning, she sends me out on Saturday morning!"

The Revealer cast a glance his way. "You'll be all right."

Entering the large sliding glass doorway with the words "entrance" and "exit" boldly emblazoned above it, Don heard a friendly greeting from a white-haired, blue-vested gentleman who long ago had worked in a factory. "Welcome to Walmart!"

Don lifted his hand to wave as he grabbed the plastic handle of a shopping cart. When he pushed it, one wheel had a mind of its own and swerved left while the other three went right. Don sighed as he continually adjusted the direction of the cart.

The Revealer, in an almost teasing tone, said, "Now Don, is that little rubber wheel really something that should be bothering you?"

Don stopped pushing. "It is pretty ridiculous that it's bothering me, isn't it? I just don't want to be here this morning."

As Don continued to finagle the obstinate cart toward the pet supply aisle, they passed the beauty department. Don saw a young girl, clad in ripped jeans with a green shirt that was hanging off her right shoulder. The purple-haired young woman had a small diamond stud nose ring firmly implanted in her right nostril and many gold, dangling earrings tumbling from her stretched earlobes. The rest of the black accessories draped around her could only be described as goth.

She looked up from a tube of mascara she had been studying and saw Don. He attempted to smile, but probably came off a little bit creepy. She scrunched up her face, making a nonverbal statement of "get away from me." Don jerked his head, looked straight ahead, and thought, "Oh, my, that went well."

The Revealer responded, "What did you expect? You were looking at her as if she was an oddity instead of trying to see her heart."

"But did you see how she was dressed? I guess I just don't get it," Don feebly said.

"Don, if you truly want to minister to people, it is not about 'getting' them. It is about hearing her heart," said the Revealer.

"OK. What's in her heart? I'm really curious," Don said sincerely.

"She has a sweet heart, but she's been hurt. She wants to demonstrate an individuality that expresses that she doesn't care what others think, but secretly it hurts her when others disapprove."

"But then why does she have purple hair and all those rings and earrings and nose rings and stuff, who knows where?" Don waved his hands around in the air.

"Her father berated her as a child, yet she still sought his attention. It bothered him when she wasn't dressed like he thought a frilly little girl should dress. That hurt her deeply. Sadly, she's still seeking attention from men who will love her not for how she is dressed, but for who she is inside."

A pensive look crossed Don's face. "That's why, when she saw me, she gave me a funny get-away-from-me look. I was coming across as judging her and putting her down."

"You people are interesting creatures," the Revealer continued. "When you want someone to help you, you turn them away. There are times when you want someone to come closer to you, but you push them in another direction. Too many times, people don't understand each other because you're sending mixed messages and aren't trying to listen to each other's hearts."

"I know that I don't always take time to learn someone's heart, but instead have just pushed them away," Don said.

"It's easier to try to stereotype people instead of learning their hearts. It's easier to lash out in a hurtful manner, instead of stepping back and examining what is going on in their hearts," the Revealer said lovingly.

"Like Sabrina in the hospital? Because her family started the church, she thinks that is what gives her value?" Don asked.

The Revealer continued with His lessons. "Sometimes, people are closer to their biological families because they know each other's hearts. There are times when the blood of family is thicker than the blood of Christ."

Don gripped the cart more tightly. "We know the hearts of our families and extend more grace to them because they have extended grace to us."

"Yes, when we know each other's hearts, grace and mercy are easier to dispense," the Revealer answered.

"Should I go back to the young woman and smile at her?" Don wondered.

"Why don't you leave her alone? She thinks you are an old weirdo," the Revealer admonished him.

"Old weirdo? I'm not that old!" Don stammered.

In the pet section aisle, lined with massive bags of Purina and Alpo dog food, Don filled the cart with dog supplies, including a black leather leash and red plastic water and food dishes. Don turned to place a rawhide chew treat in the basket when a young man walked by and gave him an unsettled feeling.

The Revealer carefully watched Don's reaction as the angry man, not much older than Don, stood near him. He was dressed in a t-shirt covered with profanity and expressed an attitude that could only be described as hate. Don didn't know whether he should smile, nod or ignore him, picking through the dog treats on the shelf.

The abrasive man was clearly filled with resentment. He shot a defiant look toward Don as if to say, "What's your problem, man?"

Don froze, certain he could sense an evil presence. "Revealer, what is going on in his heart?"

The Revealer answered calmly, "Why do you ask?"

Don made sure that his eyes were fixed on the items on the lower shelves. "I don't know, this guy just seems like something is wrong. I know I'm supposed to be trying to understand hearts, but something isn't right here. I'm sorry, but I think this guy is evil."

The obnoxious young man sneered at Don and brushed closely by him as he exited the dog treat aisle. Don let out a relieved, "Revealer, I'm not trying to be mean, but that was a little scary."

The Revealer started slowly. "You were right to be scared. Not every heart is filled with pain or purity. There are people whose hearts were so emptied by hurts that they decided to fill them with evil."

Don's eyes widened as he interrupted. "Do you mean that his heart was evil?"

"Yes," the Revealer answered, matter-of-factly. "There are those who worship and intentionally serve the enemy. The saddest part for Us is that we know the enemy will just use them and throw them away. Nothing breaks the heart of the Father more than when one of His children gives his heart to the enemy."

"I can't begin to imagine how hurt You and the Father and Son would be," Don said.

"You have no idea." Compassion poured from the Revealer.

Don perked up. "I have an idea. What if I go talk to him? I can tell him that God is more powerful than the devil."

The Revealer raised his hands with his palms toward Don. "Slow down. You are no match for the enemy. The enemy knows that he has no power compared to Us, but there is a time and a place. That young man's time will come soon."

"Can you tell me what's going to happen to him?" Don asked.

"No, it is not for you to know, but the enemy will not have that young man's heart for long," the Revealer said confidently.

"With so many hearts filled with hurt and evil, and doubt and pain, how do You and the Father handle it?" It was a statement more than a question.

"We love," assured the Revealer, "and when people need grace and mercy, We love even more."

"On behalf of all people, thank you for that love. Thank you for loving us, even though we don't deserve it."

The Revealer's face glowed. "You are welcome. We don't always hear 'thank you' but We see your hearts."

"So, what is going to happen in that angry young man's life?" Don pressed.

"It's not your concern," the Revealer said.

"I guess we are a lot like this cockeyed wheel. You and the Father and Son want us to go one way, but we go the other," Don said.

"Yes, people and shopping carts have a lot of similarities: You can be a squeaky wheel, crash into each other, and carry a lot of baggage," the Revealer said.

Don wasn't sure whether that was divine humor, but he did process how true he found those words. Passing by the beauty section, dodging the large cardboard containers holding overstocked items such as toothpaste and hair color, Don saw a man and a woman speaking animatedly in the greeting card section to his left.

Out of curiosity, Don steered toward them to hear what was going on. Surely, they were excited about something and Don was merely snooping. The Revealer inquired, "Is someone being nosy?"

Don spiritualized his response. "You are teaching me about people's hearts and I see that this couple is excited about something, so I'm just getting closer."

"And you're nosy," the Revealer repeated.

"You always take her side against me," the wife complained sharply.

"Honey, no, no. You just take it that way," the husband said, defensively.

Don parked his renegade cart near the endcap, which contained balloons and discounted holiday celebration cards, to hear their conversation. The couple standing just a few feet away from him had been married for 18 years. They were childhood sweethearts who had decided to spend the rest of their lives together after he spent four years serving his country in the Air Force.

They had a good marriage, but there was one area of contention: his mother. The husband's mother was the matriarch of the house, since her husband had died at an early age from lung cancer. She was not shy about presenting her opinions and if one disagreed with her, it stunned her to no end.

The man had two brothers and a sister. The mother shuffled around to live with them on a rotating basis. Now was this couple's turn, and his mother was the frequent object of dissension. It was not that the mother was bad, but she frequently pointed out the flaws of the wife to her husband, and usually within range of her hearing.

"The carpet was not vacuumed enough. Dirty dishes sat too long in the sink. Why isn't she taking care of you better?" These were just a few of the repetitive rants that the wife endured. Generally, the wife would flash an outward smile toward her mother-in-law, but, internally, she imagined taking a metal spatula from the kitchen and conking her on the head with it.

"But it's her birthday," pleaded the husband.

"I don't care if it's the birthday of the Pope," snapped the wife, leading Don to believe maybe they belonged to the Catholic faith.

"Honey, she is in her mid-60s. We have to get her something nice."

One could see the ire rising in the wife's blue eyes. "Almost 70, but she is going to outlive all of us because she has nagged us to the ground."

"Well, I wouldn't exactly call it nagging," the husband whimpered, "more like strong suggestions."

Don thought the wife was going to jump out of her skin. "Strong suggestions? I'd like to give her some strong suggestions, like jump off a bridge."

"Honey, you don't mean that," the husband said, trying to convince himself more than her.

"I'm sorry. I think if we just get her a card, that would be fine," contended the wife.

"But she really wants that espresso latte machine." The husband lowered his eyes to look at his wife more directly. That wound up his wife even more. "Yes, I know what she wants. Believe me, I know what she wants. That espresso machine is almost $300. We have a coffee maker and it's nice."

The husband tried to calm his wife, but was failing. "Yes, but it doesn't make the cappuccinos that she likes to have in the morning."

The wife laughed. "She could go live at Starbucks and then she could have all the cappuccinos she likes. They might even put a squirt of whipped cream on it to cover up her mustache."

The husband shook his head. "Now you're getting mean."

"I'm sorry, honey. It is just hard to live with her. You go off to work at the Post Office, but I'm with her every day for the eight hours you are gone," whined the wife.

The husband tried deductive logic. "It's only for three months, then she'll go to my sister."

The wife folded her arms. "Three months is a long time. Then, we will have an overpriced latte machine that we won't use sitting on our kitchen counter, taking up space."

"Mom will use it when it's our turn to have her live with us," reasoned the husband.

"Please don't remind me that she will be coming back again. I'm trying to deal with her being with us now," pleaded the wife.

The husband playfully flirted with his wife as he scooped her into his arms. "Just think, once she's gone, it will be just you and me."

"Hmmph, if we make it," the wife replied.

"We will make it. I love you."

She kissed him. "I love you, too. Let's go get that dumb, overpriced coffee machine."

"You're the best," her husband grinned.

They hugged and reached for each other's hands as they walked toward the small appliance section.

"Wouldn't it be wonderful if every couple's disagreements ended like that?" Don said to the Revealer.

"Yes. Why did you want to hear what they were talking about," the Revealer asked?

"I thought You knew all things," Don shot back.

"We do know all things. I want you to know why you did it," responded the Revealer.

Don considered his reply. "I guess I wanted to see whether I could see their hearts when they were arguing. I mean, really see them, not that they were mad at each other, but to see deeper than their present emotions."

"Do you think that sometimes our hearts can be overcome with pressing emotions, those even stronger than what is normally in them?"

Don really was processing. "Well, every now and then Debbie and I aren't on the same page, so our hearts can get crowded with mixed emotions, but down deep, there is a great love for each other."

"You're right, and this even extends to the relationship of people with the Father. They love the Father, but allow other things to crowd in," explained the Revealer.

"Is anything in my heart crowding out the Father?" Don asked genuinely.

"Only you can answer that, but if there was anything that was getting in the way of you and Us, I would say something about it."

"Just like that couple, I don't want anything to ever come between me and You," Don said with relief.

The compassionate face of the Revealer exhibited mercy and exuded a peace that Don soaked up.

Returning to the checkout lanes, they passed the numerous bins of bagged sugary candy and DVD movies, marked down to two for $5. Don noticed that the Revealer lagged behind a few steps. "Is everything all right?"

"Yes, the Father and I have been talking and it seems He wants to give you another gift. One that will be wonderful but heartbreaking."

Don's curiosity consumed him. "What kind of gift?"

Slowly, the Revealer opened it up for him. "The Father wants to give you the privilege of actually seeing what's in the hearts of others until we leave the store."

Don couldn't contain himself. "That would be fantastic!"

The Revealer raised His hands and cautioned, "Slow down. It is a gift, but also a burden."

Don was hurt. "But You know I have really grown these past few days. I can handle it."

Again, the Revealer seemed to be in a distant place. "OK, Father, as You wish."

Don felt a nervous energy well up; he didn't know whether the Revealer's response was good or bad. At that precise moment, an older woman walking to Don's right caught his attention. What happened next, Don would never be able to truly put into words. It was as if she were in slow motion, but it happened so quickly. Don actually saw—not heard or interpreted or learned from the Revealer, but actually saw—this woman's heart.

Don's body recoiled. With each heartbeat he was able to see inside her soul. The elderly woman smiled at Don and he saw a joy that filled her soul. Her heart beat with the joy of the Lord. Don was able to see that she had traversed through some deep valleys, but that the Lord was always with her.

As they neared each other, she once again smiled and said, "God bless you."

Don felt paralyzed but was able to feebly get out, "Uh, God bless you, too."

Don turned to watch her as she walked past, and then a scowling young man caught his eye. Inside his heart, Don saw volcanic anger, spewing toxic gas and shooting burning lava into the sky. Don wanted to help him but found himself immobile.

Don felt the Revealer's hand gently but firmly guiding him toward the checkout lane. He looked at another lane and saw a young couple staring at each other, their hearts beating with impure thoughts. Don saw both of their hearts completely immersed in hot-blooded lust. As they teased each other, Don had an idea they soon would be acting on what was occurring in their hearts.

The Revealer interrupted. "Put your items on the conveyor belt, Don."

He was quickly shaken out of seeing the couple's amorous intentions. "Oh, OK. I was just a little surprised by what was in their hearts."

The Revealer nodded his head. "I noticed."

"Paper or plastic?" asked the woman in the blue Walmart smock.

Don looked at her and finally caught himself. "Paper, please."

Don's attention was seized because when he saw her heart, it was filled with self-loathing, as if she felt that she had no value. Don stepped back to get a good look at her. She seemed to be a nice person, not overly attractive, but cute. She appeared to be a regular person trying to make ends meet.

Don couldn't figure out why it seemed as if she hated herself. The Revealer whispered in Don's thoughts, "It breaks the heart of Us when Our children have such low self-esteem."

"That will be $28.35, please," the cashier said.

Don snapped back to reality. "Sure." Don paused, but continued, "I just want you to know that you are doing a really good job and I appreciate it."

The stunned cashier replied, "I don't know what you mean, I'm just doing my job."

"Yes, but you're being professional and not everybody can deal with all the people that you see in a day," said Don encouragingly.

She could not hide a smile that seemed to radiate from the core of her soul. "Thank you."

Don noticed that her heart warmed a little to the message, "Someone cares and has noticed."

As Don packed the bags of dog supplies into his cart, he looked at her name tag. "Sara, thank you and keep up the great work!"

She waved her hand. "I hope you come back again." It wasn't just a standard customary greeting; she meant it.

"I will."

As Don and the Revealer walked toward the exit, they passed a Subway restaurant, the customer service center filled with lines of customers, and a nail salon. Everywhere Don looked, the hearts of people were revealed to him. Bitterness, scorn, happiness, joy, apathy, and sorrow were flowing from the hearts of those he passed.

Don was overwhelmed by the revelations. He didn't know what to think and his own heart seemed to be beating irregularly. He felt bad when he saw pain and he felt good when he saw contentment. He wanted to hug the couples holding hands with their hearts full of peace and to hug the people whose hearts were burdened with pain and hurt.

"The Father only let you have that gift for a brief time because if you had it for any longer it would have consumed you."

"But is that what You and the Father and Son see all the time?" Don asked.

"Yes, from the very beginning until the very end, we see everything that has happened and is going to happen," answered the Revealer.

"I have so many questions, Don said. He found himself drawn into a new understanding and awe of God, and then his mind raced ahead at breakneck speed.

"I'm sure you do. Let's get in the car and we'll talk on the way home."

EIGHT

Don grasped the beige-covered steering wheel and looked straight ahead. He felt the Revealer staring at him. "Are you all right?" the Revealer asked.

Don couldn't answer. Suddenly, he was engulfed with emotion. He felt tears streaming down his cheeks and all his thoughts cried out, "All that hurt, all that pain." But in a complete contrast, Don found his heart jumping up and down when he remembered those whose hearts held peace and joy and hope. "There was happiness," he thought.

Don felt as if his emotions were like a yo-yo. One minute, his heart was filled with so much sadness for others, but, in another, he felt joy for those who knew what happiness was all about.

The Revealer took hold of Don's seat belt and helped him fasten it. "This is why the Father and I discussed you having that gift."

"Gift, yes, it was a gift. I mean, it is incredible to see people who are filled with bliss, but it hurts more deeply than I have ever hurt for those who are just miserable," Don confessed.

"Yes, it does." The Revealer said.

Again, tears, crashing like a waterfall, overtook Don. He sobbed as he saw the hearts of the hurting people again and again. Don pressed his head on the steering wheel. The Revealer put His hand on Don's shoulder, consoling him.

Don then bolted upright. "Why aren't we in the church helping all those people? Why aren't we reaching out to them? Why aren't we grabbing hold of them by the shoulders and shaking them until they understand that they don't have to have that much pain?"

The Revealer squeezed Don's shoulder one last time before he released his grip. "Don, that's what the church is supposed to be doing."

"But why aren't we?" Don demanded.

Don wiped the tears from his cheeks. "I guess because we are so wrapped up in ourselves, we don't realize that everybody, everywhere, has issues of the heart. I guess we are so focused on the situations we find ourselves in that we don't stop to think about what others are going through."

"Don, why do you think the church is not helping more?" the Revealer asked.

It seemed as if the Revealer's intensity increased. "So, what does that mean to you? What are you going to do about the hurts in the hearts of others?"

Don felt his heart warm. "I need to focus on helping people. I need to take time to hear their hearts and not just assume I know."

The Revealer pressed him. "What do you think would happen if you did this?"

Don looked at him with a new commitment. "It would help me to see the hearts of others, like You do, and also how I can help them."

Don and the Revealer sat in silence for a few minutes as people walking from their parked cars gawked and wondered about the man sitting in the Honda Accord, wiping his face. Don turned to the Revealer. "But what if I want to help, but they don't want help?"

"That's an issue that the Father and I deal with constantly. People were created to know the Father and spend eternity with Us. But when they make choices that separate us, we want to do everything We can so they can reconcile."

Don's eyes started to brighten. "That's why the Son came to earth, to do everything so that people could get back to the Father."

"That's right, Don, we created a perfect place for people and Us to spend time together. You should have seen the Garden of Eden. It was gorgeous. But since the Father gave people the power of choice, sin entered into the world with an act of disobedience."

"The forbidden fruit," Don said disdainfully. "If only Eve would have obeyed the Father's instructions."

"Don't be too rough on her. Adam was standing right next to her as she bit down on that piece of temptation," the Revealer reminded him.

"I know, I know. He should have said something, or stopped her or . . . I don't know."

"Don, you asked why the church is not doing something about those who are hurting. In many ways, the church is standing by, as Adam did when Eve chose to listen to the enemy."

Don smacked the steering wheel with a balled-up fist. "I just need to preach harder about helping others."

The Revealer posed a question to Don: "What if you modeled it more? People can't always hear what you are saying because what you're doing is screaming at them."

Don grasped the steering wheel again. "That's the old adage: People don't care how much you know; they want to know how much you care."

"Now you're getting it. The first one you need to preach to about helping others is yourself."

Don regained his composure and turned the ignition key to start the car. Driving home, Don continually remembered all the hearts he had seen. "But shouldn't I have run to the people who were hurting and tried to help them?"

The Revealer knew that Don was second-guessing himself. "Don, this was a learning experience. Learn from it. Plus, it does people no good to focus on what could have been or should have been. People spend so much time looking back that they're not moving to where the Father wants them to be."

Don meekly argued, "But maybe I could have done some good."

"Don, people cannot change one thing that has already happened, but they can change everything that's going to happen. You had this gift for a brief time to make a difference in the future. That's why the Father is always saying 'go.' Go into the world and make disciples. Go toward the future, learning from the lessons of the past, to make your present one that honors the Father," the Revealer said.

The drive home seemed to be a blur as they passed by the unwavering trees along State Route 50. Jostled by driving over the parallel railroad tracks, Don passed by the church and thought about tomorrow's service.

"We'll get to that later, but now get home because Debbie needs help and you forgot that Eldene and Lowell were coming to dinner," the Revealer said.

Don hated to admit that the Revealer was right, but He always was. "You're right," Don conceded.

As he stopped the car in the driveway of the parsonage, Don got out and asked, "Are you coming in with me tonight?"

"Don, I have always gone in with you. Remember that you," and He emphasized you, "are never alone. But, yes, I'm coming in and later, we will go over your sermon."

Don turned the door handle and was instantly bombarded not only by two rambunctious children, but also a galloping, miniature whirlwind barking behind them. "Daddy, Daddy!"

Don wrangled both of them in his arms. "I'm going to see what is going on with Mommy and then we are going to play a game, so go pick one out."

Shouts of glee filled the entryway of the house, and the excitement was contagious. "Hi, honey. Is there anything I can help you with since we are having people over for dinner?" Don offered.

"You remembered that we were having company. That's nice. I seem to have it all under control. We'll be having pot roast and potatoes and carrots for dinner. Of course, it was the food that Eldene brought over yesterday as she was 'dusting.'" Debbie grinned. "But if you could take care of the kids while I wrap things up that would be wonderful."

"Sure, I can do that," agreed Don.

"Oh, by the way, did you get everything on the list at Walmart?"

"Yes, and a lot more," Don responded, once again thinking of the hearts of people.

Opening the oven and peering into it to check the pot roast, Debbie asked, "What do you mean?"

Don hesitantly tried to put into words what had happened at Walmart, so he looked over at the Revealer. "Honey, what do you think you would see if you could see into the hearts of other people? I mean, really see?"

Debbie straightened up and started mixing the salad for the meal. "Wow, that's a great question. I imagine you would see a lot of hurts and joys. Many people hide so much from others, but we can't hide our hearts, especially from God."

"She's right," Don thought.

The Revealer reinforced Don. "I know she's right. I told you her heart was pure."

Debbie stopped mixing the lettuce, shredded cheese and crusty croutons for a moment. "It would definitely be interesting if you could see the hearts of others. It would probably make me cry."

"It did me," Don meant to say only to the Revealer, but realized he spoke aloud.

"What do you mean, honey?" Debbie looked away from the plastic salad bowl.

The Revealer concurred, "Yes, what do you mean?"

Don cast a wide-eyed-I-can't-tell-her look at the Revealer. "I imagine I would cry if I really knew how much people are hurting."

Debbie turned back to the counter to continue her culinary presentation. "It would be neat, too, if we could see the happiness in people. I mean, there are times when the joy of the Lord with people is evident on their faces and in their eyes, but we, people, are good fakers. We hide behind a lot of things."

The Revealer agreed. "How true that is."

Don walked closer to his wife, wrapped his arms around her, and teased, "What if you could see the passion in their hearts?"

Debbie laughed. "Oh, my. Right now, the only passion that is filling my heart is to get dinner ready and for you to keep the kids and your dog out of my hair."

Don squeezed her arms in a loving embrace, "Oh, it's my dog already. I knew it!" As Don nuzzled into and inhaled the fragrance of his wife's hair, he whispered, "Maybe later, I can see some passion in your heart?"

Debbie friskily pushed back. "If you don't get out there with the kids, you're going to see some anger in my heart."

Don raised his hands and slowly backed away. "OK, OK. No need to threaten me." He went to find the marauding troupe made up of lively children and a high-spirited puppy.

As Don left the kitchen, Debbie called out, "By the way, Eldene is bringing her brother, Bill, and his wife, Ruth, to dinner also."

Popping his head back into the kitchen, Don said, "Bill and Ruth?"

"Yes, you remember them. You met them when you officiated at the funeral service of Eldene's oldest brother, Tim," Debbie reminded him.

"That's right, nice people. I'm surprised they are coming; they don't have too much to do with 'church people,'" Don mused.

"Well, what a great opportunity for us to show how good the Lord is!" Debbie beamed as she bit into a carrot plucked from the pot of roast beef simmering in the oven.

Don turned toward the living room. "Now, where are those wild children running around?"

A chorus of squeals accompanied Erin and Nathaniel as they raced down the hallway. "Daddy, look at what we taught Stretch." They stood in front of the elongated puppy and shouted the command, "Stretch, sit."

Stretch lifted his big brown eyes, the ones that seemed to be too big for his pointy-snouted face and appeared to smile at the kids. "Stretch, sit!" Again, Erin barked the order, this time raising her little hand and motioning him downward.

Just then, Don saw the Revealer move toward Stretch and the dog seemed to be watching Him. The Revealer knelt down and started petting the dog, gently placing him in a seated position. Both kids shrieked, "He did it, he did it! Did you see Daddy? He sat down!"

Don laughed in agreement. "Yes, he did." Then, Don thought, "I didn't know that You worked with animals as well."

The Revealer stood. "Remember, We created all things. Besides, We have used animals frequently. Remember Balaam's donkey? Sometimes, We've had to be extremely creative to get the attention of people."

"I know that's true," Don concurred.

"Daddy, we have the game ready in the living room. Let's play before Mr. and Mrs. Moffit get here for dinner," Erin suggested.

"Let's go! Last one has to put the game away when we are done," he said, and a stomping stampede scampered toward the living room. Don looked back at the kids and the little legs of Stretch trotting, and he saw the Revealer engaged in hot pursuit.

As they all plopped down on the floor next to the scattered Candyland game, Don cracked to the Revealer, "I didn't think You would be running."

"Don, We have been running after people since the beginning of time," the Revealer shot back.

After collecting the game pieces and retrieving all the colored cards and neatly stacking them in a pile, Don and the kids started their adventure as they traversed through Candy Cane Forest and Gumdrop Mountain. Nathaniel loudly moaned when he got stuck in a cherry pitfall in the Molasses Swamp, while Erin clapped her hands in delight as she forged ahead.

As Don moved his tiny yellow game piece forward, he paused and reflected on how blessed he was with his family. Giggles and chuckles filled the room and he glanced at the Revealer. "I am really blessed, aren't I?"

"You are more blessed than you know," the Revealer agreed.

A serious thought ran through Don's mind. "Will we have tough times when they get older? I mean, I've heard horror stories about teenagers rebelling."

"Don, enjoy them now. And when tough times come for you as a father, remember that you have a heavenly Father who will help you," the Revealer assured him.

"Is there Candyland in heaven?" Don joked.

"It is a perfect place, isn't it?" the Revealer teased.

Don cocked his head to the side and he made an interesting observation. Sometimes when he asked the Revealer a question, He did not directly answer it. Don's thoughts were interrupted when the Revealer spoke to him. "That's because sometimes, We want you to figure it out and sometimes, We will show you things later."

Just then, Erin drew the card that allowed her to enter the Candy Castle, and she won the game.

"That's not fair," pouted Nathaniel. "She always wins."

"Hey, buddy, she's a little older so that's OK," said Don.

Nathaniel was not finished being a sore loser. "When can I get to be older than her so that I can always win?"

"What's happening in his heart right now?" the Revealer asked.

"He's upset because he didn't win, but he's also being impatient," Don answered.

"Exactly!" the Revealer exclaimed. "Patience is not one of many people's greatest attributes. But never forget everything is on the timetable laid out by the Father. Everything happens when it should and when the Father wants it to."

Don shifted his weight. "Yes, but that's hard because we want everything when we want it and, when something doesn't happen, it makes it easy for us to think that You and the Father and Son aren't working."

"That misconception has been around forever. Don, never forget that We are always working, many times in ways that you will never know on this side of eternity."

"Everyone go wash your hands. The Moffits and Sorrels should be here any minute," Debbie bellowed from the kitchen.

Erin quickly rose to her feet and smugly said, "I don't have to put away the game because I won."

"Daddy, look at her. Just because she won, she thinks she's a big deal." Nathaniel said, sticking out his tongue.

"Hey, hey, don't do that. And Erin, when we win, we need to be nice," Don corrected both of them. "I'll clean up the game because you two have to go wash your hands for dinner."

"I'll beat you to the bathroom," Nathaniel challenged his sister and a foot race began between the children and the awkward dachshund.

Don boxed up the game and turned to the Revealer. "It should be interesting with Bill and Ruth here. They are nice people, but generally they stay away from church and people who go to church."

The Revealer looked intently at Don. "Remember, there is a reason for everything."

Just then, the doorbell rang and Debbie rushed to the door, drying her hands with a dish towel. Don stowed the game in the closet and joined his wife as they welcomed the dinner party into their home.

"Hello, come on in. We're glad you are here. Please, let me have your coats," Don offered.

Lowell, Eldene, Bill and Ruth peeled off their light jackets and handed them to Don, while Eldene grabbed hold of Debbie and hugged her. The kids made their way to the group and Debbie introduced them to their company.

"Kids, you know the Moffits and here are Mr. and Mrs. Sorrels. Mr. Sorrels is Mrs. Moffit's brother, Nathaniel, just like you're Erin's brother," Debbie said as she tousled Nathaniel's hair.

Nathaniel chirped, "Mr. Sorrels, did your sister, Mrs. Moffit, always win at every game, when you were growing up?"

Bill laughed. "She still wins at every game we play now," as Eldene gently punched him in the arm.

Erin gave her brother an icy look. "Nathaniel, you are supposed to say, 'Nice to meet you.'"

Ruth smiled. "Those are very polite manners."

Debbie retreated to the kitchen to make one last survey of the meal and to ensure it was ready. As she did so, she motioned for the kids to follow to help her.

Don invited his guests to the living room to have a seat. "Bill, Ruth, we are so glad that you joined Lowell and Eldene. How are you doing?"

Bill settled into the couch. "We're fine. We've never been in the home of a preacher before."

Ruth glanced over at him as if to warn him to be careful. "Bill, behave! We don't want this young man to think we are uncouth."

Eldene snorted. "Bill has been uncouth since he was born."

Bill stuck his tongue out at his older sister and Don thought he was having déjà vu. "Bill and Ruth, we are honored that you came to join us. We love Lowell and Eldene."

Eldene modestly waved her hand. "We kind of like you guys, too."

The Revealer interpreted this. "It is hard for some people to say that they love each other, but you can see it in her actions."

"Yes, we know Eldene and Lowell love us," Don said. "But I would love to know what's going on in Bill's heart right now."

The Revealer said, "Have patience and you will see."

"What do I call you? Pastor, preacher, rabbi?" Bill asked.

"Most people call me pastor, but you can call me whatever you're comfortable with," Don said.

"We call our pastors, Pastor," Eldene firmly said.

Bill took the hint but decided to be a little defiant. "OK, preacher."

With the kids jumping up and down, Debbie announced dinner was ready and asked the group to come sit around the table, which was covered with a burgundy tablecloth that had once belonged to Don's mother.

Eldene was the first one to the dining room, asking Debbie if she needed help bringing anything from the kitchen to the table. "Thank you," Debbie responded, "but I think I have it under control."

Eldene was not one to be told not to help, so she barged into the kitchen, checking to see what she could carry to the table.

Bill shook his head. "There's my shy sister."

With the table stocked with plates filled with tossed salad, a huge serving tray of scrumptious pot roast, two bowls overflowing with buttered potatoes and cooked carrots, and hot rolls just out of the oven, everyone sat down.

When they all settled in, Don proclaimed: "Let's have a word of prayer. Dear Father, thank You for this food and thank You for those who provided it for us. Thank You for my wife who prepared it and, Father, I thank You for our guests tonight. We are very blessed because You are very good to us. Amen."

A chorus of "Amens" was thrown out, but Don noticed that Bill had not contributed to the close of the prayer and looked off into space. "Bill, can I get you something?" asked Don.

"No," Bill answered. "Do you really think that God is very good to us?"

"Bill!" Ruth said sharply. "Don't be impolite."

The Revealer spoke to Don. "Listen to his heart."

"He's fine," Don said to Ruth. "That's a great question. Bill, do you think that God is good to us?"

Bill was about to say something, but muttered, "Just never mind."

Eldene had never been backward, which Don and Debbie had learned meant "shy" in this neck of the woods. "Now, Bill, you opened the barn door, so you'd better go back and bring the cows in," Eldene said.

Don assumed she meant for him to keep talking. "Please, Bill, what were you thinking about?"

"Well, a lot of things just don't make sense. Good people get hurt and bad things happen. So is God good to us?" Bill asked.

The Revealer walked behind Don and placed His hands on his shoulders. "Bill, that is a great question and one that I asked God about just the other day," Don said.

Bill seemed to be intrigued. "You mean, you wonder about things like that, too?"

"Of course, Bill. It seems as if every time God answers a question for me, three more pop up. But this is what I know: We don't, and can't, understand everything that's happening right now, but there will be a time when we will know and it will all make sense."

"I hope so, preacher. I hope so."

"Maybe, if you came to church, you'd have some of your questions answered," Eldene said, pointing a finger at her little brother.

Bill giggled. "She has been after me since you arrived here, preacher, to come to church. I did like what you had to say at my brother's funeral, but I'm just not a church person."

It was now Don's turn to giggle. "That's all right, Bill. When Jesus was here, people didn't think He was too much of a church person either."

"Enough sermons!" Eldene interjected. "We're going to have one tomorrow. Everyone, enjoy this wonderful food that Debbie made."

"We were blessed by the wonderful food from the Moffits," Debbie said. Eldene waved her hand dismissively.

The rest of the conversation during the meal covered topics like the flat tire of the church float during the Memorial Day parade, the new mayor of Bedford being a Presbyterian, and the buck that Bill's grandson had bagged earlier in the month. All enjoyed the meal and the company, and soon the visitors collected their coats as they stood by the door.

The kids politely waved good-bye to the Moffits and Sorrelses, as Bill dispensed some brotherly advice. "Hang in there, Nathaniel. Having a sister can be tough at times."

Nathaniel rolled his eyes. "Tell me about it, Mr. Sorrels!" He turned and bolted into his room, but not before he stuck his tongue out at his sister again.

"Lowell, Eldene, thank you. We greatly appreciate you and love you," Don said, as Debbie leaned forward and embraced Eldene.

Eldene deflected the sentiment once again. "We didn't do nothing." She wagged her finger at Don. "You get to bed early. You have to preach to us in the morning."

"Yes, ma'am," Don said.

Bill offered his hand to Don. "Who knows, preacher? You might see me in church sometime."

Don's face lit up. "Bill, Ruth, we would love to see you in church."

Ruth leaned forward and surprised Don by hugging him. "Thank you so much. Sometimes Bill can be forward, but you're very nice."

Don thanked her and Debbie embraced Ruth, letting her know she was a precious person. The visitors turned, headed out the door, and climbed into Lowell's Lincoln Continental. Don and Debbie turned on the outside porch light and huddled together in the doorway as they waved good-bye to their company.

Once they were all in the car, Lowell backed out of the driveway and Don and Debbie retreated inside.

"Honey, I'll take care of everything," Debbie said. "It's Saturday night, and I know that you spend time with your Sunday sermon now."

"I'll get to it. Let me help you. We have a lot of dishes."

Debbie sweetly responded, "I'll get it. I want to hear a word from the Lord tomorrow."

Don pulled her into his arms. "Have I told you how blessed I am because of you?"

Debbie tenderly pushed him away. "Yes, and now go and get to work."

Don pretended to pout as he grabbed his jacket and started out the door. Don's usual Saturday night routine was to have dinner with his family and then go to the church for any last-minute sermon preparation and prayer. This was usually a special time for Don because there were no interruptions or distractions, just him and the Lord. Of course, with the Revealer present, Don was curious about tonight.

As they pulled into the church parking lot, Don turned to the Revealer. "Are You going to look over my sermon? Are you going to correct it and make any changes? You know, You could write one for me. I know it would be good."

As they walked up the church steps, the Revealer said, "Don, we have been writing a sermon since Wednesday night, don't you think?"

Don thoughtfully nodded his head as he unlocked the church door.

"Yes, I've learned a lot."

"What have you learned?" the Revealer said, pressing him.

Don halted in his tracks.

"I've learned so much, so much about the hearts of others. I had no idea that people felt like that. Like Bill tonight. I think that he has a good heart, but is afraid of trusting the Father because of so many questions."

"You are learning to listen to people's hearts," the Revealer said, complimenting Don. "Good. And, yes, Bill's heart is good, but being good won't get you into heaven. You have to know the Son, who ushers you to the Father."

"Hopefully, Bill will come around. I like him."

"Maybe sooner, rather than later," the Revealer said mysteriously.

They descended the steps toward Don's office and opened the door. Don cautiously scanned the room, not sure what to expect. As he took off his jacket, he walked behind his desk and started to outline the lessons he had learned about the hearts of others and his own. The Revealer stood near him, showering him with a presence of peace.

Don had prepared many sermons, but when he was able to look up and see the Revealer standing next to him, a supernatural feeling tingled throughout his body. The Revealer noticed that Don was looking in the mirror.

"Remember, Don, that even when you can't see Us, We are always here."

For hours, Don felt surrounded by legions of angels, crowding into his office agreeing with his message. He sensed the presence of the holy apostles Peter, John, and Thomas walking in a harmonic bond with him. Don reflected on how the Bible talks about being surrounded by a great cloud of witnesses and he believed their manifestation was a reality.

NINE

Sunday came, the day of worship, the day when God's people come together to pray, worship, and hear a message from the Lord. Sadly, many churches have become divisive battlegrounds, where the wounded and weary merely go through the motions as tradition dictates. Other religious gatherings try to cast a wide net so that everyone fits in, as their theology is wider than the Mississippi River and gets just as muddy.

The Huron Church of God was neither a confrontational site nor a social club camouflaged as a church, but was like the majority of American churches, simply existing and plateauing before plunging into decline. Don knew that God wanted him to serve there, but after three years of butting heads over unexplained policies and unspoken protocol, he had grown frustrated.

Today, however, renewed enthusiasm ran through his veins. For the first time in what seemed to be ages, Don looked forward to standing before the people of the Lord as God's messenger.

Don had set his digital clock radio's musical alarm for 6 a.m., even though Sunday School didn't start until 9 a.m. with the morning worship commencing at 10 a.m. Don liked to spend some time alone with the Lord in preparation before preaching. Even though Don was exasperated in many ways, he still treasured presenting the Word of God.

Looking in the mirror, Don adjusted his dark red tie, pulling it closer to his neckline. As he stepped out of his bedroom into the hallway, the Revealer stood there waiting for him.

Don was startled. "You scared me! I wasn't expecting to see You yet."

"You didn't think that I would miss the biggest opportunity of the week to see people gather in the name of the Father, did you?" asked the Revealer.

"No, of course not. I just didn't expect You this early," Don responded.

They walked down the hallway into the kitchen, where Don poured the coffee into the filter before placing it in the Mr. Coffee machine and

93

grabbing a couple of pieces of bread to toast for breakfast. Don leaned back against the counter as he waited for his meager meal and inquired, "Is today going to be any different than any other Sunday at church?"

The eyes of the Revealer grew wide.

"Let me ask you that question. Is today going to be any different?"

Don nodded his head, as the pieces of toast popped up.

"Yes, I believe so. I have learned a lot these last few days."

"Good," the Revealer smiled. "Now is the time to implement those lessons."

The aroma of the coffee spread through the kitchen as Don chewed on his toast and sipped the steamy, hot brew. Normally, he was by himself when he practiced his Sunday morning ritual, but today he had company.

Don placed his coffee mug in the sink, wiped the excess breadcrumbs off the counter, and walked to the closet by the front door. Putting on his jacket, he turned to the Revealer and said, "It's time to go to church, unlock the doors, make sure the bulletins are in the right spot so Stan can pass them out, and check to make sure everything is ready."

The Revealer followed him at a leisurely pace and it seemed to Don that He was keeping a little more distance from him than normal.

"Is everything all right?" Don asked, his curiosity piqued.

"Yes, why do you ask?"

"You just seem to be hanging back a little this morning, and this is the morning when I feel I need you the most," Don explained.

"I know and I am with you, but you seem to be relying on your own strength instead of mine, so I won't crowd you."

"I don't mean to come off that way," Don said with a frown. "I'm just a little nervous. What if I have not learned the lessons You and the Father want me to learn? What if I don't listen to any hearts today, but just roll over people like a bull in a china shop?"

The Revealer wrapped his arm around Don's shoulder as they walked to the car.

"You're going to be all right. Remember, We never seek to be impressed. We just desire your obedience."

Don felt encouraged as he climbed into the car.

"Normally, I run through the church and check to make sure everything is OK, then I go to my office to practice my sermon."

"I know," the Revealer said with a grin.

Don parked in the spot farthest from the door, to leave the closer spaces for older members so they did not have to walk as far. When Don unlocked the glass front doors, they entered the house of worship.

"Sundays are special to me," Don said, inhaling deeply.

"They are special to Us, too," the Revealer agreed.

Don took off his jacket and sprinted up the steps to the sanctuary to get the tri-fold bulletins and place them on a table near the entrance, ready to be passed out. Then he went through the sanctuary just to make sure it was presentable, so that he did not get chewed out after the service.

The Revealer walked up to the chancel area and stood behind the large wooden pulpit. Don looked up.

"You look good up there," he said. "You should be there more often."

"Remember Don, that's what We want as well," the Revealer said, smiling.

The Revealer and Don descended the stairs to his office and Don sat down behind his desk. He picked up his 10-page typed manuscript and read over it a couple of times. Don was stunned when he glanced at the long rectangular mirror hanging on his door and saw the Revealer standing behind him, with His hands raised to the heavens. It appeared as if the face of the Revealer was glowing. Don was taken aback. He didn't know whether he should speak and, besides, he would not have known what to say.

Don felt consumed with the presence of the Living Lord. An inexplicable energy jolted through Don's body, his heart pounded with the force of a runaway jackhammer, and his soul was strengthened in a manner he had never felt. The Revealer then placed both hands on Don's shoulders and communicated without speaking. He was praying over him with more than words. Don felt the very essence of heaven descending upon him.

The Revealer then lifted his hands and told Don, "It's time. Go."

Don stood up. His legs were a little wobbly, but inwardly he felt refreshed. He grabbed his blue suit jacket from the spindly coat rack where he kept his collection of two other suit coats. Don flashed a smile at the Revealer. He was ready.

As Don arrived at the top of the stairs, Stan walked through the front door, took off his weathered Carhartt jacket, and arranged it on a metal hanger. Stan saw Don and approached him.

"Have you been thinking about what we talked about Wednesday night about Mike's Amens?" It really wasn't a question. It was Stan's way of saying, "you'd better do something about the matter."

Don stuck out his hand warmly to shake Stan's hand. "Stan, what's really bothering you? It really can't be Mike's amens, is it?"

"What do you mean?" said Stan, looking shocked.

Don pumped his hand up and down in a friendly fashion. "Normally, you don't get too bothered about things like this. What's going on?"

Stan drew his shoulders back a little. "Well, Pastor, I have been having a hard time with my right ear and the doctors can't seem to help me. So, when I hear something loud on that side, it sort of sends a sharp pain through my head."

"I understand that," Don said sympathetically. "Can you sit on the other side of the aisle?"

"But, Pastor, I've always sat where I sit. Since I came to this church, I haven't been in any other pew," Stan protested.

"Yes, but is your friendship with Mike and spending time in worship not worth you moving to a different area?" Don asked, tilting his head to the side.

"I guess so, Pastor, but if anyone asks, I'm going to tell them that it was my idea," Stan said.

Don laughed and picked up the bulletins, which featured on the cover an image of the world surrounded with pictures of missionaries. He handed them to Stan, who nodded his head. Out of the corner of Don's eye, he saw the Revealer giving him a thumbs-up.

Debbie and the kids arrived just a few minutes before Sunday School. Don walked the children to their classes in the basement and Debbie headed to the sanctuary, where the older adults gathered for class, taught by Eldene. She had told a former pastor that she only wanted to teach her class for one more year, but that had been 17 years ago. Anytime she brought up the idea to Don, he changed the subject and she taught for another year.

Normally six children and twelve adults showed up for Sunday School. Don usually poked his head into the children's classes and walked up to the sanctuary to sit by Debbie for Eldene's class, which was taught from the quarterly booklets.

Sunday School lasted for 45 minutes and Charlie Clark, the worship leader, buzzed around, making sure that the person assigned to sing the solo before the sermon was there. If he couldn't find the soloist, he scurried around frantically, loudly moaning as if he was in great distress, searching for another singer.

Today, Charlie saw Crystal in the sanctuary and called out, "Are you ready for today, hon?" She waved back, assuring him that he could relax. Don moved through the sanctuary, greeting people and telling them that it was good to have them in church this morning. Don tried not to do it, but every Sunday, he surveyed the people in an attempt to determine the number in attendance.

It was almost 10 a.m. and the morning worship service was about to begin when Don was caught by Julie.

"Pastor, will you be using the divinely inspired King James Version today in your sermon?" she asked.

Don wanted to say, "No, I'm using the heathen NIV," but chose not to. Instead, he smiled and kindly said, "Julie, you know I prefer the NIV, so I'll be using it today."

Don turned away from her to walk to the chancel, but then turned back toward her. "Julie, while we may disagree on the versions, I appreciate how important the Word of God is to you." She leaned back in the padded pew and started to fan herself.

There were almost 40 people finding their seats, greeting each other, asking whether they were working hard or hardly working, and waving at people across the narrow aisle. Tom saw Stan sitting on the right side of the church instead of the left and snapped, "What's wrong with you? Why are you sitting over there?"

"I can sit anywhere I want," Stan said. "I can hear God better over here."

Don caught the conversation and wanted to loudly say "Amen," but decided not to do so.

Lowell sat in his normal spot, the fourth pew back on the left side, but as Don stepped up the three steps to the chancel, he failed to see Eldene. Don thought that was unusual, until he saw Eldene turn sideways as she was ushering her brother, Bill, and sister-in-law, Ruth, into the sanctuary.

Don raised his hand and waved at Bill, who winked and grinned at him. Charlie began playing the prelude on the old mahogany Kimball upright piano, which was mostly in tune. He plunked his hands upon the keys and then nodded his head toward Don, indicating that it was time to start.

Don stood and welcomed the worshippers and asked if there were any announcements that anyone wanted to bring. Don didn't like this perfunctory act, but he had been told that announcements were always open and sometimes they didn't have anything to do with the church. As usual, Margaret stood up. "I just want to remind everyone about the ice cream social next week at the fire station to support the Daughters of the American Revolution."

Don nodded his head in agreement and quickly looked at Charlie to begin singing. In the midst of getting settled and the service beginning, Don had lost sight of the Revealer and he started searching the room for Him. In the last pew on the right, Don spotted Him sitting by Chloe, who was in her early 20s and one of the youngest attendees, as she wrestled her 6-month-old baby, Emma. Emma helped Don preach at times, as she loudly interjected wails or unsettling shrieks.

During their corporate singing, Don looked out at the people and saw two sisters, Alice and Nella Hancher, leaning toward each other, talking as if they were sitting on a park bench together. There had been times when Don had thought, "I should stop the service and ask if we're interrupting them."

As that thought ran through Don's mind, he heard the Revealer ask, "Upon whom are you focusing? Them or Us?"

Don had been chastised and he knew it. "I'm sorry. I got distracted. I want to focus on You and the Father and the Son."

The ushers gathered to take the offering and waited for Stuart Simpson because he usually made a big production of taking money out of his wallet so everyone could see him plop the green bills into the circular brass plates. "At least he gives," Don thought.

After the offering, Crystal marched forward and sang "In the Garden." Don listened intently. Not every note was on key, but he knew that her heart was sweet and she meant well.

Now was the time for the sermon and as Don approached the broad pulpit, he placed his hands on each side of it. Normally, he was frustrated when he stood up because he was distracted by someone looking out the window or rolling their eyes as if they didn't want to be in church. But today was different.

The first few words out of Don's mouth caused the congregation to gasp.

"I'm sorry. In some ways, I have failed you as your pastor."

Immediately, several people jumped to the conclusion that he had either embezzled the paltry finances of the church or that he was about to confess a juicy affair. Either one would have caused a major ruckus and been fodder for good gossip for weeks.

"I have learned many things these last few days, things about other people, but most important, things about myself," Don continued. "In seminary, they provide tools like how to study the Bible or how the Levites offered the sacrifices, but they didn't teach us this one thing. That is how to see the hearts of others.

"These past few days, I have spent time intentionally trying to hear the hearts of others, to see how I can help. It has not always been easy and I have not always gotten it right, but I'm trying. Another important lesson God has taught me is to watch my own heart. Sometimes, I think things that I shouldn't. Sometimes, I'm not compassionate when I should be. So, I am making a commitment to you today that I will do my best to see your hearts."

Alice and Nella's mouths dropped open. Mike let out a boisterous "Amen," while Stan, who had his arm extended along the edge of the pew, was beaming from ear to ear. Debbie cocked her head as if she were listening as closely as she could. Something was going on with her husband and she liked it.

"So, I'm not going to preach to you today, I'm just going to talk to your hearts," Don said. "We are created by an awesome heavenly Father, who loves us with all of His heart. But because of sin, we were separated from Him. Our hearts grew cold and emptiness flooded in as if a concrete-walled dam had burst open. We try to fill our hearts with so many things, but we get so crowded. Anger, bitterness, resentment, hurts fill us up and eventually our hearts are so full that we don't have any room for God."

Eldene nodded her head in affirmation. Julie held her King James Version tightly, but hung on her pastor's every word.

"When we get to a point where we realize that we have so much in our hearts that God is not in there, we have a couple of choices. We can either keep going the way we're always going. We can dig in, like that mule that got loose from the Renner's barn that Margaret told us about last Wednesday, or we can turn our hearts over to the Father. When we do that, He comes in and will give us the peace He has for us. Not only that, but God wants us to have joy as well. I know for a fact that God laughs with us."

Baby Emma was unusually still and Chloe didn't have to wrestle with her this morning. Tears welled up in Mike's eyes and on the other side of the aisle, Stan's heart was filled with peace.

Don looked out and noticed that Bill had leaned forward with his head bowed. For what seemed an eternity, Don stared out at the people and saw their hearts. He saw the heartbreaks of some while he noted others were flooded with a contentment that could have only come from God. Don saw deep pain in some of their hearts, which nearly caused him to break down in tears.

Don stepped away from the pulpit and walked off the chancel, shocking some of the people.

"God loves you. He is here and He wants to fill up your heart. So today, if there is anything in your heart that is blocking you from receiving the peace and hope that God has, then today is the day to get rid of it and welcome him in. . . ."

Before Don could continue, Chloe slowly rose to her feet, holding Baby Emma close to her chest. She started walking toward Don and, for a second, he didn't know what to expect. As she neared the front of the small sanctuary, Margaret stood up and held her arms out to hold the infant. With one motion, she took Baby Emma and tenderly embraced Chloe.

A holy stillness overtook the sanctuary and Don noticed that the Revealer was standing up, pacing back and forth behind the pews. He was not walking fast or in a menacing manner; He was filling the tiny room with His presence. Chloe finally arrived in front of Don and said, "I want my heart to get rid of all my junk and I want God in it."

Mike shouted "Amen" as tears rolled down his face and Stan grabbed the white handkerchief out of his pocket to pat his cheeks.

Don looked out at the congregation. "Does anyone else want to come to meet God and have Him fill your heart?"

At that point, Eldene gasped audibly as Bill stood up and inched past her. Lowell grabbed hold of his hand and they locked eyes. Bill said, "Lowell, I need to get my heart right."

Lowell nodded, unable to speak; he was overcome with joy.

Bill exited the pew and announced: "Pastor, my heart needs the Lord. I need to get saved."

Overwhelmed with the presence of the Lord, Don's knees felt like Jell-O. Bill walked up and stood next to Chloe, the single young mother. Don looked around and extended the invitation again. "Today, we can make sure our hearts are filled with the Lord."

Two more people, Ron Pratt and Jason Wade, who were visiting the church from out of town, slowly rose and joined those in front.

Debbie moved forward and placed her hands on Chloe's shoulders in a loving manner. Mike and Stan looked at each other, then stood and strode to the front, placing their hands on the shoulders of Ron and Jason in affirmation. Don moved in front of Bill, who held out his hands to Don. As he clasped them, a flood of emotion overwhelmed Bill and Don and tears flowed.

After he regained his composure, Don led the four who came forward to the Lord and their hearts were filled. Chloe turned and tightly held Debbie as Margaret rocked back and forth and told Baby Emma that her momma was going to be all right. Stan and Mike offered manly embraces to the other two who had come forward and walked back to their pews with arms on each other's shoulders.

Bill paused before he returned to his seat. "Pastor, can I say something?"

"Absolutely," Don replied without hesitation.

"I have run for a long time away from God because I tried to have it all under control," Bill said, his voice cracking. "But this preacher . . . I mean, my pastor, has helped me to see that only God is in control and I am happy that I can say that today my heart belongs to God."

Several people raised their hands and two shouted "Hallelujah." Don looked at Charlie, who was not sure what to do next, so he ran behind the old piano and started playing the Bill Gaither chorus, "I'm so glad that I'm a part of the family of God."

People swayed and turned in their pews to shake hands and lean forward to embrace each other. Don looked out and saw the Revealer walking among the people, laying His hands on them. His face was cast toward heaven. Don's heart overflowed and he realized that it was all about the heart. One heart at a time. Not a big church, not a big budget, not a lot of church vans, not a television show with commercials asking for donations, but the heart.

Charlie was in full swing and started playing "Amazing Grace." Don looked back and saw Eldene fussing over Bill, alternating from punching him on the arm to grabbing hold of him, to wiping the tears from her face. Ruth stood next to Lowell and appeared to be in disbelief. Don saw her heart and knew it would not be long before she came to know the Lord.

Charlie started playing the hymn "How Great Thou Art," and a hallowedness enveloped the sanctuary. Later, when Don relived that moment, he described it as divine. The heart of the little church in Huron had been ushered into the very throne of God and He blessed them.

"Thank you for coming today and may God bless you all!" Don announced, still shaking with a sanctified spirit. He walked past the nine pews, with five on one side and four on the other, extended his hand to Debbie, who caught up with him, and went to stand by the glass doors to greet the people.

Debbie gripped his hand tightly. "I love you," she said.

Don replied, "I love you with all my heart," and she squeezed more.

People milled around longer than usual. Generally, when Don pronounced the last "Amen" of the last prayer, people rushed as they headed to Bedford to get a seat at Perkins' restaurant before the Baptists arrived. But today it seemed as if they stood around and talked, the men patting each other on the back and the women swaying back and forth, hugging their friends.

As Mike left, he was filled with energy. "Pastor, we had church today!"

Stan was not far behind him. "It didn't even bother me today when Mike said Amen."

Don noticed they met in the parking lot to go eat lunch together at the steak house in Mitchell.

Chloe filed out. Debbie caressed Baby Emma's head and told Don, "Honey, we are going to watch Baby Emma a couple nights a week so Chloe can have some time for herself. Is that all right?"

"Absolutely," said Don, a wide smile creasing his face.

When Alice and Nella sauntered out, they were closely huddled and Alice griped, "People sure acted up today. That was horrible." Nella jumped on the mean bandwagon. "Pastor, we really don't care for all that carrying on during church today. God wants us to be quiet."

Don wanted to say, "Is that why you two talk during the whole service?" Instead, he bit his tongue and genuinely smiled at them. "I hope that you two ladies have a wonderful day and may God bless you."

As the two fuddy-duddies left the church, Debbie elbowed Don. "I'm sure those weren't the first words that wanted to come out of your mouth."

"No," Don grinned, "but God has put us here to serve Him through the thick and the thin,"

Debbie laughed. "And through the loud and the quiet." Don squeezed her.

Eldene slowly sidled up to Don, pretending to be angry. "There you go, Pastor, bringing the Holy Spirit to the church. Look what happened!"

Then she burst into a smile, with her eyes flashing and her face expressing joy. "I'm so happy!"

"I am, too," Don said, hugging her. "And, yes, it was nice having the Holy Spirit with us today."

As Don said this, the Revealer spoke to him. "I'm always here but people aren't ready to see Me. Today they were."

Lowell extended his hand and pulled Don in for an awkward embrace; Lowell was not known for embracing.

Bill almost jumped into Don's arms. "Preacher, I mean Pastor, I want you to know that when I came in here this morning, I was going to listen to you, but that was about it. Then God spoke to my heart. Thank you."

"Bill, you can call me whatever you want, because now you are my brother," Don said. They embraced again.

In the joyous commotion, Debbie pulled Ruth to the side, away from the excited group, and said, "Ruth, if you would ever like to talk about the Lord, I'm here for you."

Ruth's face beamed. "I would like that. Can I call you soon?"

"Anytime."

Ron and Jason, the visitors who had asked the Lord to fill their hearts, told Don they would be moving on next week, but now their hearts were right with the Lord.

Don asked if he could pray over them. "Father, take care of my two brothers and lead them where you want them to go. Let their hearts always know you."

"Thank you," said both men, as tears welled up in their eyes.

Julie still clung to the King James Version, pressing it close to her chest, "Pastor, you didn't use the King James Version, but I believe God was here today."

Don smiled. "Yes, He was."

Margaret slowly walked down the three steps from the sanctuary, taking one step at a time. "Pastor, wasn't that wonderful today? By the way, it wasn't a mule that got out from the Renner's the other day, it was a donkey."

Don laughed. "Thank you for enlightening me and by the way, thank you for holding Baby Emma while Chloe came forward."

Margaret waved her hand to show she was happy to help.

"Honey, I mean Pastor, anytime anyone wants Jesus in their hearts, old Margaret will be there to help."

"I believe that," Don said, and he knew he saw her heart.

After everyone was gone, Don and Debbie stood by themselves in front of the glass doors in the lobby. Lowell and Eldene took Erin and Nathaniel with their entourage to Dairy Queen in Bedford to celebrate her little brother Bill's salvation. Debbie drew close to Don. "What is my heart saying to you?" she asked.

"Let me lock up and I will meet you at home," Don smirked, mischievously.

"Don't be long," Debbie said and headed to the blue Ford minivan, the Stouts' other vehicle.

Don walked up to the sanctuary and caught himself reliving the service. Don had not seen the Revealer for a while and when he turned around, he noticed that He was sitting in the back pew.

"Wow. That's all I can say," Don exclaimed.

"You are learning to see the hearts of people."

"Yes, but not everybody. Alice and Nella left complaining and I'm sure that they're on the phone now, complaining to anyone who will listen."

"Don, there were four people who gave their hearts to the Lord, many others were filled with God's presence and all you can think about is those two?" chided the Revealer.

"I know. All I can see in their hearts is meanness." Don sat down next to the Revealer.

"Yes, never forget, not everyone allows the Father to control his, or her, heart. So, you focus on those who do, love those who don't, and continue to be honest with your own heart," the Revealer wisely said.

"Yes, that's a lesson I need to learn," agreed Don.

"And you will keep learning it again and again."

Don started to unknot his tie. "What did the Father think?"

The Revealer's face glowed with a holy light. "He was pleased. Now, go home and spend time with your wife and I'll meet you tomorrow."

Don stood, took off his suit jacket, ran to his office to hang it up, and quickly drove home.

TEN

At 5:12 p.m., Don and Debbie's time for themselves was broken up as the kids burst through the front door. Nathaniel jumped around ecstatically, jabbering about how many cows he was able to pet, while Erin calmly tried to teach him that the proper name was "cattle."

Don popped his head out the front door, raised his hand, and waved to Lowell and Eldene. He would have invited them into the house, but he knew after they spent time with the Stouts' bundles of energy, they wanted to get home to relax.

"Well, what else did you two do?" Debbie asked.

Shouts of glee rang out. "We went to Dairy Queen and ate a large ice cream cone," Nathaniel said. But since she was the older sister, Erin needed to make full disclosure. "Yes, but he did spill a little on the table and Mrs. Moffit had to go and get a lot of napkins to clean it up." Nathaniel tilted his head and gave his sister a mildly menacing look.

"That's OK, buddy," Debbie said. "Sometimes we make a mess. We'll play a game, take baths and get everything ready for tomorrow. Erin, you have school. So, go pick out a game in the closet."

They returned with the game Operation, which takes a steady hand to pull tiny plastic organs out of a poor patient. If a player isn't successful, a loud buzzer sounds, usually causing the player's hand to jerk back.

After a few games of jolting shocks, buzzers, and much laughter, Debbie told the kids, "Please put the game back and then it's bath time."

Eyes rolled and quickly movement went into slow motion, but the kids grudgingly obeyed. As she picked up the board game, Erin said, "I really like Sunday nights, but the one bad thing is when you wake up, it's Monday morning."

"Don't worry honey," Don joked, "it's going to be like that for the rest of your life. Plus, tomorrow after school, Nathaniel and I will pick you up and we'll go to the park in Bedford." Eyes opened wide and hands clasped in joy showing Don the kids liked that plan.

Erin was first in the bathtub. Debbie washed her hair and wrapped her up in multiple fluffy towels as she dried her. Next was Nathaniel. He wanted Stretch, the new puppy, to join him, but Don knew that would result in a flood of Biblical proportions spilling through every square inch of the bathroom.

After a short family devotion time, reading a Bible story from a well-worn book, the kids headed to bed. As Debbie corralled them into their bedrooms for the night, she turned to Don. "I'll tuck them in tonight." Don let out a sigh of relief. It was his night to do the honors, but he still found adrenaline pumping through his veins from the powerful morning worship service.

When she finished putting the kids to bed, Debbie returned to the couch, leaning against its right arm as she stretched her legs and extended them over Don's lap. "How are you feeling, honey?" she asked sweetly.

Don realized that they hadn't talked about how the morning worship had gone or about what had happened. The alone times they were able to share were far and few between, so they concentrated on other things.

Don massaged his wife's legs. "I think today went really well."

"You could tell that the Holy Spirit was present," Debbie said, cooing as Don rubbed her feet.

"Yes, He was present," Don said pensively. "What if that happened every week? I mean, wouldn't it be wonderful to see people love each other and get saved often?"

Debbie cocked her head back. "Isn't that what church is supposed to be about?"

Don felt he was hedging. "Yes, but so many Sundays, I'm either hearing about problems or who is mad at whom, or that I haven't done something perfectly."

"Honey, that is going to happen as long as there are people. But today was different because, Don . . ." Debbie paused, reluctant to hurt his feelings. "Don, something was different about you today."

Don abruptly stopped his massage and at first felt a flash of hurt, mixed with a tiny bit of anger, shoot through his being. "What?"

But he caught himself because he knew it was true. Since he had been spending time with the Revealer, he tried to see the hearts of others instead of their exterior airs and behaviors. And Don truly attempted to catch his own heart when he focused on himself more than God.

"You're right," Don said, looking her straight in the eye. "This past week has stretched me."

Debbie pulled in her legs, nestled up to Don, and snuggled as closely as she could. "I've noticed that. Is there anything I can do?"

Across Don's face came a smile that spread through the depth of his soul. "Debbie, I love you and you do more for me than I could ever ask. Someday, we'll talk about this week."

Don leaned forward and planted a sweet, loving kiss on his wife's lips. They watched a couple of television shows together as they curled up with one other and then went to bed.

Don drifted off to sleep, thinking about Bill coming forward to the varnished altar and could not help smiling. At 3:30 a.m., Don was suddenly awakened from a deep slumber. The first thought that raced through his mind was for the safety of the kids. Are they OK? Are they all right? Don was puzzled because he didn't know why he was wide awake.

Don's mind reeled as he tried to reconcile the thoughts crowding it. "You know, the reason why the service was so good today was because of you. You really should be preaching somewhere else. These people don't realize your talent." Don was stunned as these ideas kept echoing in his mind.

The barrage continued. "But you know, if you really were that good of a minister, you would be in a different church. Maybe you're the problem." Don's mind spun faster, like a berserk turntable spinning out of control. "You know, this whole Revealer thing is just a figment of your imagination. You've been under a great deal of stress."

Don realized that he was under spiritual attack and surprised himself as he spoke audibly. "The Revealer is real and that is why the service went well today." Debbie stirred a little and groggily mumbled, "Are you talking to me, honey?"

Don patted her shoulder. "No, honey, I was just having a bad dream, that's all. Please go back to sleep."

She turned over. Don closed his eyes and concentrated on the scripture verse of Matthew 11:28, "Come to me all you who are weary and heavy laden and I will give you rest." Don prayed, "Father, I think the enemy is coming after me tonight, so please watch out for me and allow me to get back to sleep." Soon, he slipped into slumber.

The next morning as Don drove Erin to school, he thought about the conflicting ideas that had run through his head the previous night. Erin chattered away about the lessons she was going to learn today and wanted to make sure that her father didn't forget that they were going to the park after school. She seized Don's attention when she firmly said, "You promised us, Daddy."

"Yes, we're going to the park after school," he said, as they pulled into the loop of Sawyer Elementary School. Erin's school was in Mitchell, which was about eight miles from Huron off State Route 60, which branched off of State Route 50. Bedford was less than seven miles north on State Route 37.

Arriving at the school with kids flooding in, Erin tugged on her My Little Pony backpack as she exited the car. "Remember the park!" Don smiled as he nodded his head and watched his little girl being greeted by a young school aide, who was enthusiastically waving her hands at all the passing parents.

Don turned the steering wheel to the right and was startled to see the Revealer, now sitting in the front seat. "Oh, my, you scared me."

"Many times, when the finite have connected with the Infinite, the first reaction is to be scared. That's why many times the angels had to greet people with the words 'Don't fear.'"

"I'm glad You're here," Don said. "Something weird happened to me last night."

"I know," the Revealer acknowledged.

Don shot him a glance that said, "Why didn't You do something?" but then continued speaking. "It was like I started to become proud of how wonderful I am, but then I started beating myself up."

"Those are common tactics of the evil one," said the Revealer. "He likes when the leadership of the Father's people think they are the reason people have access to Him. He likes when pride overtakes their hearts, because they quit focusing on the Father and start to rely only on themselves."

The Revealer continued his counsel. "The enemy also likes to beat up ministers because, if he can discourage a minister, he or she may quit. And if they don't, then that discouragement can trickle down to the people and affect them."

Don listened intently. "All I could think to do was think about scripture."

The Revealer reassured him. "That's good, that's very good, but why didn't you call on Me?"

Don almost stopped in the middle of the road. "I didn't even think about it. I hadn't seen You since the morning service . . ."

"Don," the Revealer said, "We are always with you."

"I know. I'm sorry. I should have called on You," Don said.

"Next time—and I'm sad to say that there will be a next time, and a next time, and a next time the enemy will attack—call on Me. Scripture is good, too, but never forget that the Father and Son and I are only a whisper away."

A calming tranquility settled over Don and he etched deeply in his mind that he needed to call on the Revealer when the enemy attacked.

"And Don, the Father is always working," the Revealer said. "There are so many things happening behind the scenes that He is doing. The Father is setting up what needs to take place at exactly the right time."

"What do you mean?"

"You'll see," the Revealer remarked casually.

They pulled into the driveway of the parsonage and as they were walking to the front door, a tousled, wild-haired, 4-year-old pushed the door open. "Is it time to go to the park yet, huh, huh?"

Don grabbed him by his waist and hoisted him over his shoulder like he was carrying a burlap sack of potatoes. "Not yet, buddy. When Erin is done with school, we'll pick her up and then go to the park."

Nathaniel giggled and wiggled as his father carried him into the living room and gently placed him on the couch, where he started tickling him. "Don, you have a phone call," said Debbie.

"Who is it?" Don asked between the playful clutches of his squirming son.

"It's Pastor Liddle from Bedford."

"Thanks, I'll take it in the bedroom," Don replied as Debbie handed him the white cordless phone.

"Good morning, Pastor Liddle. How are you? Is everything all right?"

"Don, I'm well and everything else is well, too, thank you for asking. I just wanted to call today to tell you I heard you had a great service yesterday," Liddle said.

"Thank you, Pastor, but how did you hear about our service?"

"A young man named Ron made a proclamation of faith yesterday," Liddle explained.

"Yes," excitement rose in Don's voice. "He and another man were visiting because they live out of town but are working in the area."

"Yes, I know," Liddle chuckled. "Ron is my wife's cousin. He stopped by our house on Saturday and mentioned that he and a friend might find a church in the morning. When I asked them where they were staying, he mentioned Washington, so he was right by you. Since he was close, I suggested he go to your church and, from what I hear, the Holy Spirit showed up."

Don couldn't contain himself. "That's true, Pastor Liddle. You should have seen it. It was amazing. We actually had four people come to know the Lord and people even shouted 'hallelujah!'"

"Wow, at the Huron church. That's wonderful!" Liddle said encouragingly.

"Don, I know there have been times when you have felt frustrated, but remember, God is always faithful and if we wait upon Him, He always comes through," said Pastor Liddle in a wise manner.

"Pastor, this past week I've learned a lot, even during the ministers' meeting," Don said.

"All of us should be learning. Well, Don, I'll let you go, but I just wanted to call and tell you I'm proud of you."

"Pastor Liddle, that means a lot to me. Thank you." As Don and Pastor Liddle said goodbye to each other, Don was uplifted.

"It feels good when we seek to encourage each other's hearts, doesn't it?" the Revealer said.

Don, still looking down at the phone, answered, "Yes, it does. The heart of Pastor Liddle encourages me."

The Revealer nodded His head. "As well it should. Pastor Liddle has faithfully served the Father through seasons of stress and majestic moments on mountaintops. He is a good man and it would be wise for you to continue to learn from him."

"Absolutely," Don agreed.

The rest of the day, Don and Nathaniel mowed the grass, a major undertaking since Nathaniel's toys posed as land mines dangerously scattered throughout the green landscape. Of course, every 15 minutes, Don heard the same question repeated from his eager son: "Is it time to pick Erin up to go to the park?"

When they finished mowing and placed the red Sears Craftsman mower, which he and Nathaniel had ridden all day, back into the shed, Don concentrated on his fidgety son. "Let's go wash up and then go get your sister."

Nathaniel exuberantly erupted, "Yeah, it's about time."

After cleaning up, Nathaniel quickly hugged his mother as she rearranged some of the groceries that Eldene had brought during her "dusting" and surged toward the front door. "Honey," Don said, "it's time to get Erin and then we're going to go to the park in Bedford."

Debbie stopped her inventory, gave her husband a peck on the lips and replied, "Have fun and make sure you wear them out."

Don leaned in for another kiss. "I'll do my best."

When the front door swung open, Nathaniel darted toward the backseat of the car and stood there, waiting for Don. His father opened the door and Nathaniel crawled into his "big boy" car seat. Nathaniel hated to be strapped while they were driving; he was too easily distracted to sit in one place. Plus, he was not happy that his sister had graduated to a regular seatbelt because she sat upright and did not move around when the car was in motion.

Easing through the loop of the sprawling brick school, Don waited his turn as a part of a caravan methodically crawling forward as little people ran from the side of young aides and to their cars. Erin jumped up and down when she saw her family's Accord and raised her right hand as she pointed it out to the aide standing next to her.

As Don inched to a stop, Erin ran over, opened the passenger side back door, maturely grabbed the seat belt, clicked it into place, and sat straight up. Nathaniel watched her accomplishment with jealousy. Don could see the wheels turning in Nathaniel's head about wanting to tease his sister, so he quickly said, "Hi, honey! How was your day?"

"It was good, Dad. Did you know that all sides of a rhombus were equal?"

Don was taken aback for a second. "Honey, I might have at one time, but I'm not sure I knew it now."

Nathaniel's face was scrunched up. "What is a runaway bus?"

Carefully taking her time, Erin explained, "It's a parallelogram, right Dad?"

Don looked over at the Revealer, hoping He would bail him out. "Honey, I'm not sure, but if that's what the teacher told you, I'd believe her."

Driving north toward Bedford, the kids sang along with a CD that Debbie had created for them to pass the time in the car. Erin and Nathaniel were loudly singing, "This little light of mine, I'm going to let it shine" and "I have joy, joy, joy, joy, where, down in my heart." Soon they arrived at Wilson Park to unleash some of their energy.

Wilson Park was nicely laid out, with a section for kids that contained a tall, winding plastic slide, several rows of leather-strapped swings, and a large brown-and-red playhouse fashioned in the shape of a wayfaring ship, complete with a rotating boat's wheel.

Nathaniel wriggled with all his might to get to the action, while his sister calmly removed her seatbelt and said, "Take your time. We'll get there."

The Revealer chuckled. "She's so much like your wife."

"How true that is," Don agreed.

Once Nathaniel was freed from his seat, the kids dashed toward the large plastic play ship, which they had nicknamed "The Pirate Place." Don and the Revealer followed leisurely behind. There were several white wooden park benches on the perimeter of the playground, strategically placed so that parents and guardians could see their children at all times.

Don chose one between the "The Pirate Place" and the swings since he knew the kids would alternate back and forth between these two areas. As he and the Revealer sat, Don noticed that there were more children than were normally at the park. Usually, five to 10 kids played in the mini wonderland, but today it seemed more like 20 little people scurried around noisily.

Don slowly scanned the other park benches. He saw that they were mostly occupied by mothers, but there was one father talking excitedly on his phone to his office. The tone of his voice indicated it was not a pleasant conversation. The Revealer watched Don as he calculatingly watched others.

Don turned toward the Revealer. "What are you doing?"

The Revealer responded, "What are you doing?"

Don laughed. "How come, sometimes when I ask You or the Father a question, I get a question back?"

"We know what We're thinking, but We want people to be honest about what's going through their minds and what they're harboring in their hearts."

Don's said, "It all gets back to our hearts."

"Yes. Were you wondering about the hearts of the other adults scattered around the playground?" the Revealer asked Don.

"You know that I was," Don answered glibly.

"OK, then, tell me what is in the heart of the father on the phone, over there?"

Don studied him more deliberately. "His heart may be filled with the desire for power. He wants to be important."

"Why do you say that?" asked the Revealer.

Don's squinted his eyes. "It seems that he's arguing with someone about something work-related, and his frustration can be heard in his voice."

"OK," the Revealer pressed, "what about that woman sitting over there, the one looking down at her iPad?"

"Well, she may be so preoccupied on social media that she doesn't make time for her kids. I think those are hers over there who keep waving at her but she doesn't see them," Don said.

"Maybe, but one lesson I must teach you when you look at the hearts of others is not to impose your own perceptions and ideas upon them."

Don was confused. "What do you mean?"

The Revealer leaned toward Don to emphasize his point. "Sometimes, people think something is going on in the hearts of others and they may not be accurate. How many bad people have maliciously fooled many good people? How many good people have been terribly misunderstood and have faced negative reactions because they were misconstrued?"

Don was not quite sure where the Revealer was going. "So, was I wrong about the father over there?"

"Yes. He is not the father of the little boy with the Pacers basketball hat. He is his uncle, and he left work early to help out his sister, who had a doctor's appointment. He has an important presentation tomorrow and he hates to be away from his team, but he didn't want to abandon his sister."

"So, his heart is not filled with seeking power or prestige, but really is good. He is frustrated because he needs to be in two places," Don said, seeking clarification.

"Yes, and the woman who is staring at her iPad is Googling the effects of cancer treatment because she was just diagnosed with breast cancer," the Revealer said.

"I really got both of those wrong, but how am I going to know the hearts of others if I may be wrong in so many cases?" Don said, upset by his assumptions.

"The only true way to know someone's heart is to spend time with them," the Revealer said, acknowledging Don's frustration. "When people make snap judgments about the hearts of others, they don't know the whole story. Knowing the whole story of what people go through, have to deal with, and have gone through makes a great difference."

"But I thought when this week is over, I would be able to know people's hearts."

"This week, the Father granted you the gift of My visual presence to teach you to make an effort to learn the hearts of people. He said that I would reveal them to you, not that you would have a magic crystal ball that allowed you to peer into someone's soul," the Revealer said, chastising Don.

"Then was this week a waste?" Don replied angrily.

"I hope not," the Revealer expressed in a sad tone. "I hope you have learned the importance of seeking to learn someone's heart and the most important lesson, to know your own heart."

"I have learned a great deal about my own heart," Don muttered more to himself than the Revealer. "I'm a mess and I have a long way to go."

The Revealer reached over and patted Don's knee encouragingly.

"Don't beat yourself up. Just take one step at a time in your journey with the Father and sometimes, as you take two steps forward, you may take a step back. Don, there was a wise man who lived on earth named C.S. Lewis. You have read some of his books. Mr. Lewis wrote, 'If we only have the will to walk, then God is pleased with our stumbles.' Don, keep stumbling toward Us."

The Revealer raised His hand and pointed to Nathaniel and Erin, who were scrambling toward the row of swings, and said, "Now, go and push them on the swings and have fun."

Don stood slowly, processing all the Revealer had said. He wasn't sure whether he was doing well or not. As he crossed the playground surface of finely ground rubber, Don heard the Revealer say, "You are doing good. Just like you are walking now, take one step at a time. Take one step closer to Us."

Don looked back and felt affirmed. When he turned toward the swing, he saw that Nathaniel had tried to climb up onto one and was dangling upside down. Erin's swing was slowly rocking back and forth and she glanced at her misaligned little brother, rolling her eyes. Don raced to Nathaniel, righted him, and stood behind him, gently pushing him until his swing was swaying back and forth.

After an hour of alternating between the triangular-poled swing set and "The Pirate Place," Don told the kids it was time to go home. They groaned loudly and whined, "Can we stay just a little longer?" Don held his ground and promised that they would come back on Thursday after school.

Don and Debbie settled into their normal nightly routine of playing a game, taking baths and tucking the kids into bed. Don wanted to go to bed earlier than normal since he had planned a full day at the church tomorrow. Debbie noticed this and asked, "Are you all right, hon?"

"Honey, since last Wednesday, I'm not sure if I'm all right or not," Don said, lovingly looking at her.

Debbie was stunned by Don's mysterious answer, but didn't push him to explain.

At 6:30 a.m., Don's digital alarm radio once again serenaded him with Mercy Me's gospel hit, "I Can Only Imagine." He showered, dressed, ambled into the kitchen for coffee and two pieces of buttered toast, and walked out the door to go to the church.

Tuesday tended to be a major workday for Don as he prepared his Wednesday evening Bible Study lesson and started the process for Sunday morning's message. Today, he would research, outline and put illustrations or anecdotes in a bulleted outline, and then on Friday, he would write out a full manuscript of his message.

During one of Don's seminary classes, he had attended a seminar on "The Art of Memorization" and learned how to highlight major points of his sermon, memorizing them so he could preach without taking notes to the chancel. Don was always amused when people said that he wasn't prepared, since he didn't take any paper notes with him, but found solace knowing they were wrong.

Don opened the glass doors of the church, disentangled a metal hanger from another as he hung up his coat, and walked down to his office. When he inched his door open, he saw the Revealer sitting behind Don's desk with his hands interlocked behind His head. "Are You comfortable?" Don asked.

"Very, thank you for asking. Let's go. We have a lot of work today," the Revealer said.

"We do?"

"Yes. Isn't it exciting that you have the privilege of preaching and teaching the Word of the Father? Wow!" exclaimed the Revealer.

Don walked around the corner of his desk as the Revealer stood up, bowed in a playful manner, and motioned for him to sit in his chair.

"I like that You are excited, but sometimes I have to work hard for a lesson or message," Don said.

"Good," the Revealer grinned. "You're taking it seriously. You're not a simple talking head or a fantasy storyteller, you're imparting words of life, words of hope, words of instruction and, most important, the words of the Father."

Don realized the Revealer was right. "Yes, we're not talking about Reader's Digest or Entertainment Weekly. We're talking about Kingdom stuff."

The Revealer reiterated, "Yes, We," strongly emphasizing We. "We are presenting life. There are too many harbingers of doom and too many self-help gurus wanting to sell you their secrets, while the Father is reaching out His hands to receive you. People need to know that!"

As Don hunkered down in his padded chair, he felt as if legions of angels were surrounding him. He felt as if he were being elevated to an audience with the Father and Son. He sat back and basked in the totality of a moment in which peace prevailed and closed his eyes. He never wanted to forget this feeling. As he slowly opened his eyes, Don realized the Revealer was right next to him, His face glowing with glory.

Exuberantly, Don walked to his book-filled shelves and pulled some commentaries to begin his research, while the Revealer approvingly stood nearby. After several hours, Don had prepared his Wednesday night Bible Study about the passage in Matthew 6:21 "where your treasure, there your heart will be as well" and had his basic outline for Sunday's message completed.

Don's heart was satisfied and the Revealer warmly embraced him, filling him with joy.

"Today, you have done well," the Revealer said quietly. "Go home and enjoy your family and I will meet you here tomorrow morning."

Don turned toward the door and gripped the brass doorknob. He glanced at his desk and saw that the Revealer had settled back into Don's chair and once again stretched out His arms, bent His elbows, and interlocked His hands behind His head.

ELEVEN

Don slept soundly, but woke earlier than normal. Usually, his eyes quickly opened when his alarm clock chirped its welcome song, but for some reason today, he was conscious before that took place. As he swung his feet over the side of his bed, he felt an inexplicable nervousness creep into his soul.

Before Don stood, he glanced back at his sleeping wife and a small smile creased his face. The apprehension that woke him earlier than normal had nothing to do with Debbie or the kids. It was because today was Wednesday.

Normally, Wednesday's arrival was not a major event for Don, but today was the last day he would spend time with the Revealer. Don caught himself and thought, "Of course, this is not the last time that I'll spend time with the Revealer. I'm going to spend a lifetime with Him." But Don knew this would be the last time he saw Him this side of eternity.

Don's mind careened from one thought to another, like a ping pong ball rapidly volleyed back and forth across a net during a game of table tennis.

"Tonight, after Bible Study, that's it," Don thought. "No longer will I see the Revealer sitting next to me in the passenger seat."

As if a speeding arrow pierced Don's contemplation, he thought, "What if I don't do a good job at Bible Study? It would be terrible if the last time I spent with the Revealer wasn't done well."

Don made it to the shower. While he was rinsing the shampoo from his head, he thought, "No, I have to quit beating myself up. The Revealer said that my preparation was done well. I'm ready to teach." Feeling encouraged, Don dried himself with a fluffy terry-cloth towel and dressed.

Once again, doubts and attacks of inadequacies sprang into Don's thoughts.

"What if I've prepared something good, but someone gets me off track? What happens if I don't go the direction I'm supposed to be going?

What happens if the people don't get the point that the Father wanted me to lead them to?"

Waiting for the bread to pop up out of the stainless-steel KitchenAid toaster, Don leaned back against the counter and tried to distance himself from the fog that clouded his mind.

"No, if the Revealer were here, then He would tell me that these thoughts are not from the Father, but are assaults from the enemy to cause me to wallow in a pit of destruction."

He was on a roll.

"Yes, that's it. The enemy doesn't want me to think the Bible Study will go well. The enemy wants to tear me down so that I'll focus on distractions, instead of trying to see the hearts of people."

But gloom continued to intrude on Don's thoughts.

"But what if I do see the hearts of the people and they're not positive? What if they're coming to Bible Study to lash out at me? What if they're coming to Bible Study not because they want to learn, but merely because that's what they do, that's what they have always done, that their hearts are overloaded with tradition."

Don stopped chewing on his buttered toast.

"I have to quit thinking like this. I just need to get to church. The Revealer said that he would meet me there in the morning. I just have to get going."

He finished his breakfast and washed it down with one last swig of coffee from a mug the kids had given him for Father's Day.

Don twisted the copper doorknob to leave the house.

"What if I just stay? There are always a few jobs that need to get done around the house and it would be good to spend some time with Debbie. Besides, my lesson tonight is done. Plus, I could always spend time with the Revealer later this afternoon."

Even though the enemy was intently trying to talk Don out of going to the church, he kept walking toward the car. But the enemy was not yet finished with his sly ambush, so he started placing other thoughts in Don's mind.

The enemy knows that many times people can resist and rebuke him for a season, but after the repetitive darts continue to be flung their way, one projectile may reach its target. The enemy knows that after enough time, people wear down like a screaming child at a grocery store weakens the mother's resolve and she breaks down and lets him have that coveted candy bar.

Don looked over his right shoulder as he backed out of the driveway, when the enemy planted the biggest bombshell in his mind. "Do you really want to see the Revealer?" Don took his foot off of the gas, applied the brake and thought, "Why would I not want to see the Revealer?"

The enemy knew that Don was almost hooked and ready to be reeled in, so he planted this idea: "You know, not everyone has had the privilege of spending a week in which they were able to actually see the Revealer, don't you?"

Don hesitated as the car idled. "Of course, I realize what an incredible gift I have been given."

The enemy was just warming up.

"But why you? You're really not that important. You're not pastoring a big church. You haven't written a best-selling book on how to be a great Christian. You're nothing more than a normal guy."

Don's shoulders slumped.

"I thought about that in the beginning, but was reassured I was being granted an incredible gift from the Father because I asked for it."

The enemy sensed Don's resolve was cracking.

"Now, come on. You really don't think this was a gift, do you?"

"Of course, it was a gift," Don said emphatically.

"You know, the Father does it all the time," the enemy jabbed back. "You people think that you're special, but then He gives you a little treat and you quickly wag your tails."

Like a shark in the depths of ocean sensing blood, the enemy circled.

"Don, the Father sends the Revealer to people all the time just so they get excited, but when it really dawns on them what took place, they're disappointed."

"When what really dawns on us, I mean, me?" Don asked, his curiosity piqued.

"Yes, the Revealer may have taught you a few things but you have no idea how much He held back," the enemy chuckled. "You know, He and the Father and the Son don't want you to know everything. Look at the Tower of Babel."

"Wait a second!" Don said angrily, his defenses kicking in. "The people were scattered from the Tower of Babel because they were trying to make themselves gods. They were trying to push God out of the way."

"That's what the Father wants you to think. Let me ask you a question, Don," the enemy condescendingly said.

Don didn't reply in his mind, but the enemy moved forward relentlessly.

"Didn't you have a lot of questions this last week when you were with the Revealer?"

"Yes," Don said, shrugging his shoulders. "So what?"

"Was every one of those questions answered, Don?"

Don felt dirty when the enemy casually used his name.

"No, but that doesn't mean anything. There are many, many things that we will not know on this side of eternity. Remember, the Bible says in 1 Corinthians 'now we know in part.'"

"Yes, the Bible. But doesn't it also say in James 1:5 that God will give you wisdom, so you are supposed to know everything?" the enemy said, subverting the truth.

Don knew the enemy was correctly quoting half of the scripture verse, but manipulating the rest.

"OK, Don, this is just something I want you to reflect upon. When you were with Revealer, did He show you every person's heart?"

"Well, no, well, yes. I mean, He did at Walmart," Don said, feeling frustrated.

"Yes, Walmart," the enemy lashed out. "The Father only let you see people's hearts for a very small amount of time, didn't He?"

"Yes," Don responded slowly.

"But if He really wanted to teach you and for you to know, would he not have given this gift to you all of the time, so that you would always be able to see the hearts of people?"

This made a little sense to Don, but he said, "It's not for me to always have this gift."

"Of course, it's not, Don," the enemy snapped. "That's why I told you this was not really a gift."

Don shook his head because he had started believing what the enemy was saying. He made a conscious decision that he had to get to the church as soon as possible, and continued to back out of the driveway, then turn right onto the road toward the church.

The enemy wasn't done yet.

"OK, Don, but what about when the Revealer asked *you* what you thought was in the hearts of people?"

"So?" Don asked, puzzled. "He was teaching me to look deeply."

"Don, Don, Don," the enemy said patronizingly. "How are you supposed to look deep and see someone's heart?"

Don felt the enemy's stinging reply and said: "The Revealer taught me how our history forms our hearts and then our behavior demonstrates it."

The enemy burst out laughing.

"So, with some tricks that a first-year psychology student has mastered, you can see into someone's heart?"

"It's not a trick," Don said, driving more slowly. "It's true. Our hearts can be seen by our actions and our words."

"Yes, it's like on the children's TV show 'Barney.' I love you and you love me. Everything is that easy," the enemy teased.

Don's frustration increased.

"You're twisting everything I am saying," he said. "You're trying to get me to think the Revealer and the Father have used me as some sort of cosmic joke."

"But isn't that the truth?" the enemy said, going in for the kill. "Weren't you people just created as an afterthought?"

"No, we were created to love God because He loves us," Don said, his face flushed.

"There we go, back to the oversized purple dinosaur again."

Don reached the parking lot of the church and the voice of the enemy became softer.

"Don, I didn't mean to give you a hard time. I just don't want to see you hurt or disappointed when this Revealer thing goes away."

Taken by surprise, Don guided the car to a stop in the parking lot. He didn't know whether the enemy was being compassionate, or it was simply his own thoughts. With his mind juggling theological questions and personal questions, he felt bogged down as he walked up the sidewalk to the front doors of the church.

Don turned toward the single row of hangers, grabbed one and thought: "The Revealer was in my office the last time, but what if He isn't in there today? What if this last week was some kind of joke? What if I've just sort of dreamed that all this took place?"

So many questions, so many things undetermined, so many doubts filled his mind.

After hanging up his coat, Don turned to descend the stairway to the basement of the church. Standing before his office, he took a deep breath in anticipation and tried to assure himself: "I'm not going to be too disappointed if the Revealer isn't in there," but then he caught himself. "I'm going to be very disappointed if the Revealer isn't in there."

Don marveled at how he contradicted himself, but yet it made perfect sense to him at the time.

Don took the key out of his pocket, unlocked the door, and quickly pushed the door open. He did not have to look far because the Revealer was standing right on the other side of the door, with his hands widely extended, indicating He was about to embrace Don.

Don lingered for a second, stepped forward, and found himself wrapped in the Revealer's warm embrace. Don felt a sense of relief and peace that started from his head and slowly moved all the way down his body to his feet. He almost wept, unsure of the emotions flooding his heart.

"You have had a tough morning, haven't you?" the Revealer said. It was more a statement than a question.

"Yes, I have. I don't know what's going on." Don's body experienced deep relaxation as the Revealer hugged him one more time in an embrace that filled Don with reassurance.

The Revealer knew this was a teaching moment.

"Don, what do you think happened this morning?"

Don knew immediately when the Revealer uttered his name that it was good, as opposed to earlier when he had felt violated as the enemy spoke it.

Don walked to his desk and sat down in his chair.

"I'm not exactly sure what happened. I woke up early and all these questions and accusations started going through my mind. I didn't think I could stop them."

The Revealer sat down on the brown leather chair on the other side of Don's desk.

"What kind of thoughts?"

"Confusing ones," Don said as his eyebrows furrowed.

Kindness radiated from the Revealer.

"We know who the confuser is, don't we?"

"Yes, but I have to admit, some things made sense. There was some truth in what he spoke," Don said, slightly perplexed.

The Revealer nodded His head in agreement.

"Yes, he has always sprinkled in a little dash of truth with the lies he cooks up."

"But how do I know if it's the enemy or it's my own doubts and thoughts?" Don interrupted the Revealer. "Things that I came up with?"

The Revealer leaned in closer to the desk.

"That's a great question, Don, because sometimes the enemy receives much more credit for actions than he should for actions that aren't his. And he's also received undeserved blame when people have said, 'The devil made me do it.'"

"Yes, but how do I know?" Don laughed. "How can I fight back when I fight him? What if it's my issues coming out? How do I fight those?"

The Revealer leaned back and crossed His right leg over His left.

"Let's break that down into two separate questions. First, if the enemy is attacking you, and he will often, how can you know if it's him?"

Now Don leaned back in his padded chair, encapsulated in deep thought.

"I guess if he directly contradicts the truth then it's the enemy, and if he wants to look away from God."

"Now you've got it," the Revealer said. "The enemy's primary purpose is to get people to look away from the Father and many times he does this by. . ."

"By having us look at ourselves," Don interjected. "People are very selfish, aren't we?"

The Revealer nodded.

"Yes, so if you find yourself not thinking about the Father, what can you do?"

"I thought about a scripture verse," Don said.

"Excellent! The Word of God is your sword. Use it to cut through the web of lies the enemy tries to trap you in. But be aware: One of his greatest weapons is to manipulate scripture."

"Yes, he did that with me," Don said, his eyes opening wide.

"Yes, I know," the Revealer concurred. "But I have a question for you, Don. Why did you stop in your driveway? Why didn't you come straight to the church?"

Shame overwhelmed Don.

"I guess that I started believing the lies of the enemy, or I was trying to figure them out, or I allowed myself to get caught up in them."

"Don, you're forgiven. But never forget, it's the times when you feel the farthest from Me and the Father and the Son that are the times to run to Us. We're always with you."

"You were there, in the car?" Don asked, demonstrating his surprise.

"Yes," came the Revealer's simple but profound answer.

"But I didn't see you. I was even looking in the mirror when I was backing up."

Don was astounded.

"Yes, but your eyes were not looking to see me when your mind was being filled by the enemy."

"I'm so sorry." Don choked up as he sincerely apologized.

"Don, I told you that you were forgiven," the Revealer smiled. "Receive it."

Don gratefully accepted the grace the Father was giving him.

"But what if it's not the enemy, it's just my doubts and fears coming out?"

"That's a great question, Don. You can know by always being honest with what is going on in your heart. Always look at your motivation. Always be real because you know that people can and do fool others many times, but I and the Father know exactly what is in your heart. And so, do you."

"So, I guess I can't ever say again, 'The devil made me do it,'" Don chuckled.

"No, you can't," the Revealer grinned.

Don and the Revealer sat together, comfortably enjoying each other's company as old friends. After a season of just being together, Don looked over his lesson for that night and began to work on the multi-page manuscript for Sunday's sermon. As Don worked, he looked up at the Revealer. "Is there anything You'd like to add?"

"It looks good, but remember, even though you won't be able to see me on Sunday, I'll be with you."

Don stood and stretched his legs.

"I know, and that makes me feel good."

It was almost 4 in the afternoon, which gave Don a little time to go home and eat a sandwich before the midweek Bible Study commenced. After Don ate, he wrestled with Nathaniel and asked Erin how her day went at school. Debbie laid out a dress shirt and tie for him and he put them on.

Don usually arrived at the church around 5:30 p.m. to make sure the doors were unlocked and the lights were turned on. Normally, after finishing those chores, he sat down in a pew and dreaded what he knew was coming. But tonight, Don experienced a different sensation. He was actually looking forward to Wednesday evening Bible Study.

Mike and Stan were the first ones to arrive, and Don cheerfully greeted them.

"How is your ear doing, Stan?" he asked.

"It's a little better and I'll be all right, especially if this big lug,," he teased, pointing to Mike, "doesn't blow out the rafters with 'Amens.'"

Mike erupted in a belly laugh. "I just can't help it, Pastor. God is good."

Stan grabbed Mike's shoulder and they sat down together in a pew. Of course, Stan sat on the right side of Mike so that his right ear would not be pierced if Mike became excited.

Chloe backed into the church, as she was wrangling Baby Emma in a carrier and juggling a pink diaper bag. As Don moved to help her, Margaret raced up the steps, grabbed the diaper bag, and ordered Chloe to "get up those steps and sit down. I'll hold that precious baby so you can have a break for a few minutes."

Debbie and the kids arrived. Debbie and Nathaniel peeled off their coats and Debbie raced downstairs, trying to keep up with her energetic son. Don noticed that Erin stayed by the glass doors, peering outside and focusing on the parking lot.

"What's going on, honey?" Don asked, as he wrapped an arm around her shoulder.

"Do you remember the girl in my class that we prayed about a few days ago?" she said without looking up.

"Yes. Is she all right?" Don said, sensing Erin's apprehension.

With her big eyes, she looked up at her father.

"Yes, she's fine. I invited her to church tonight and I hope that she comes."

"Honey, I'm so proud of you," Don said, enveloping her in a hug. "I hope that she comes, too."

Tom was next through the door, followed by Julie, who again was tightly clutching her King James Bible. Erin started jumping up and down excitedly. "Daddy, I see my friend! She came!"

A blonde-haired woman, Kim Nelson, and her little girl, Rachel, walked up the sidewalk to the church and Don opened the doors for them. When the two little girls saw each other, they hugged and started giggling. Erin told her friend where to hang her coat, explained the layout of the church, and took her downstairs where the kids would meet.

Don greeted her mother in a friendly fashion. "Welcome! Thank you so much for bringing your daughter. My daughter, Erin, was really looking forward to her coming."

"You're welcome," the woman said kindly. "She has been bugging me for a while to bring her to church."

"Will you be staying?" Don asked the woman "We have a Bible Study in the sanctuary."

"No, not tonight, but my husband and I are thinking about coming next Sunday to church," the woman answered politely. "What time do I need to pick up my daughter?"

"We'll be done in about an hour, but then the kids have a snack. You're welcome to join them," Don told her.

"Thank you. I might do that," the woman said and turned to walk to her car.

It was almost time for Bible Study to start. Debbie had six kids downstairs, already coloring pictures of Biblical scenes such as David and Goliath, Noah's ark, and Jesus feeding the 5,000. Don found himself filled with joy, which was a foreign feeling for him on Wednesday nights.

Boosting his euphoric mood even more, Don heard a rustling near the back of the tiny sanctuary. Looking up from the small podium upon which he had been arranging his notes, Don saw Lowell, Eldene, Bill, and Ruth enter and lift their hands to wave at everyone. It was unusual for Lowell and Eldene to attend the midweek service since Lowell was on the board of a local co-op and his presence was always desired at the meetings for the calming effect he had on people.

Don smiled at them. "It's good to see all of you. Lowell, they let you out of your meeting?"

Lowell slowly spoke with a soft drawl. "No, but Bill said we need to start coming on Wednesday nights, so here we are."

Don glanced at Bill as he settled into a pew.

"Preacher, I mean Pastor," Bill said, "I figure that since I got saved, I'd better act like a Christian, so I have to learn how to be one."

Don choked back a lump in his throat to prevent tears from filling his eyes.

"Thank all of you for coming tonight. I know we're all busy, but it's good to come study the Bible and encourage each other."

As Don spoke, he noticed Chloe sitting with her legs crossed under her, a Bible on her lap, staring ahead intently. Margaret sat straight up, wrapping Baby Emma in a quilted blanket like a tight cocoon. As Don went to the Lord in prayer, he found himself overwhelmed with emotion because he knew how blessed he was.

Don managed to make it through the prayer without breaking down and asked the worshipers to turn to the gospel of Matthew, chapter 6, verse 21. After flipping the thin pages of his Bible, Don began to teach them.

"I know that last Sunday I talked about how important it was for us to have God in our hearts, but I want to dig a little deeper tonight. Matthew 6:21 teaches us that where our treasure is, our heart is as well."

Julie quickly raised her hand, catching Don's attention. "Julie, do you have a question?"

"No, I just wanted you to know that it's the same verse in the King James Version, in case you were wondering," she said, smiling as she looked at all the others in the sanctuary.

Don nodded his head politely and realized that he had not taken offense at her statement. He probably would have if she'd said it prior to his week with the Revealer. Don thought, "You know, when you do try to know their hearts, it makes it easier to understand them and to minister to them."

The Revealer answered him, "You're right." Don thought, "Where is the Revealer? I don't see Him."

Don thought he heard the Revealer chuckling. "Don, I'm with you, but I'm also here, standing next to Debbie teaching the little ones about Daniel in the lion's den. I love that story."

For a second, Don thought how the Revealer was blessed, watching the awe and wonder in the eyes of the children as they heard how Daniel was surrounded by scary, mighty creatures with big teeth, but was protected. Don uttered a quick prayer: "Father, never let me lose the awe and wonder of your stories."

Don's lesson defined and described different treasures and shared how they affected people. "If money is our treasure, we can know how rich we are by how much we have in the bank . . ."

Hesitantly, Bill raised his hand. "Pastor, can we talk back to you tonight? I know on Sunday; I have to sit quietly. At least, that's what Eldene told me to do," he added, as she shot him an intimidating look only an older sister could get away with. "But if money is our treasure and we spend it, won't we have empty hearts?"

Don's heart was blessed beyond measure. He loved that someone with only a rudimentary understanding of theology—even though he was not aware of that big seminary word—wanted to know more about God.

"Bill, you're exactly right," Don replied. "People have been trying to fill their hearts with so many things, but if our hearts aren't filled with God, all that will pass away and we'll have nothing."

Eldene nodded her head encouragingly toward her brother, as he winked at her because he was affirmed by the pastor.

"How can we tell what's in our hearts?" Don asked.

Margaret, shifting Baby Emma to her other arm, said, "I want to help people. Is that in my heart?"

Chloe turned to her. "Margaret, you don't realize how helpful you have been to me in church with Baby Emma. I believe your heart is a treasure." Don couldn't tell whether Margaret actually blushed or not, but he could see her heart filled with joy.

Mike spoke up. "Pastor, sometimes my heart gets so filled up with God that I just have to shout or else I think I would explode!"

Stan reached over, slapped him on the back, and said, "I know that's true, brother."

Everyone laughed. Suddenly, it hit Don that he was not on edge and frustrated. He did not feel pressured to have a perfect lesson. Tonight, he was with brothers and sisters in the family of God, and they were learning and encouraging each other together.

For a short time, Don laid out specific ways to make sure the treasure of their hearts was God, such as prayer, spending time in God's Word, serving, and engaging in other spiritual disciplines. Then Don saw the Revealer enter the back of the sanctuary and stand directly behind Ruth.

"Ruth, is God talking to you? Do you want to ask Him to come into your life and be the treasure of your heart?" Don gently asked.

Ruth stiffened and wondered whether she should tell him that what was happening in her heart was none of his business, or if she should run up and hug him. So, she sat there, until tears started streaming down her face. "I want God to come into my heart."

Bill's hand shot up like it was fired out of a cannon. "Preacher, can I say 'Hallelujah?"

Don caught himself almost speechless and nodded his head exuberantly. "Hallelujah!'" Bill's shout soon was accompanied by a loud "Amen" from Mike and, shocking even himself, Stan excitedly erupted, "Praise the Lord!"

Don asked everyone to stand and make a circle, holding hands. As those who had been separated from each other by the pews melded together in unity, Don stood next to Ruth and asked her if she was sincere about having a relationship with Jesus Christ. Her head enthusiastically bobbed up and down as Bill began to weep.

They started with a prayer of repentance, expanded to prayers of thanksgiving, enlarged to prayers of worship, then swelled to prayers of adoration at how wonderful the Lord is. In the midst of hearts connecting faithfully before the Father, Don looked up and saw the Revealer standing in the middle of the circle with His hands outstretched, blessing the people.

Time seemed to stand still, but, eventually, the small group of worshippers realized that it was after 7 p.m. when Nathaniel ran up the steps and shouted back to Debbie, "I think they're either praying or they're frozen."

Laughter, which led to hugs and the shedding tears of happiness, contagiously spread through the group. Don thought, "Son, you missed that one. We were definitely not frozen."

TWELVE

Ruth lingered close to Don after those in the prayer circle started to return to their pews and gather their belongings. Margaret was bent over, moving in full motion, scooping pacifiers and little trinkets that had spilled out of Baby Emma's pink diaper bag. Ruth, with genuineness shining in her eyes, asked Don a powerful question. "Pastor, am I saved?"

Don pulled her into a warm embrace. "Ruth, you are as saved as I am and I know that God is very happy right now."

"You can know that God is happy? How?" Ruth was amazed.

Don looked over at the smiling Revealer, who was standing at the back of the small sanctuary. "Trust me on this one."

At that moment, Bill charged up. "Pastor, we have to go to Dairy Queen in Mitchell."

"Dairy Queen? I'm not sure what you mean," Don said, stunned.

Bill very plainly told him, "Preacher, every time a Sorrels gets saved, we go have ice cream. I sure hope there is ice cream in heaven."

Don laughed. "It's a perfect place."

As quickly as Bill appeared next to Ruth and Don, a bustling Nathaniel cried out: "Dairy Queen! Did I hear someone say Dairy Queen?"

Don started to say, "Not tonight, buddy. . ." but was quickly cut off, as Debbie and Erin joined the entourage.

"Daddy, are we going to Dairy Queen?" Erin asked.

Don tried to be the voice of reason. "Honey, it's a school night and you need to get your rest."

Debbie didn't back up his logic. "Honey, I'll take them for a few minutes and get some ice cream. I mean, this is what we do when a Sorrels gets saved!"

Nathaniel jumped up. "I sure hope a lot more Sorrels get saved!"

Don knew he was overruled. "OK. You go to Dairy Queen. I have some more work to do here."

Lowell and Eldene joined the group. Debbie turned and said to them, "We're going to Dairy Queen. Would you please take the kids so I can clean up downstairs? I'll meet you there."

"Dairy Queen!" Eldene blurted out. "We just went there on Sunday."

Bill bent down and winked at Nathaniel. "That's because a Sorrels got saved, right bud?"

Nathaniel's exuberant body language agreed. "Yes!"

Eldene, pretending that she was really bothered about having to go to Dairy Queen, conceded, "I guess, if we have to go, we'll go. Kids, get your coats and load up."

Don realized that people were getting ready to leave the church, so he excused himself and rushed to stand in the tiny foyer to say good-bye. The first to reach Don was Julie. She extended her hand with her elbow locked, which made a handshake a little awkward, but Don received it and returned it gladly. "Pastor, I know we may not agree on what translation is the best, but I'm learning a lot," Julie said pleasantly.

"Julie, I'm happy to hear that, and please know that I'm learning a lot, too," Don said, encouraging her.

The Revealer stood next to Don and asked, "What do you think of her heart now?"

"She has a sweet heart," Don answered, "and I admire her for acting on her convictions about how important the Word of God should be for us."

"Don't forget that," the Revealer said, looking intently into Don's eyes.

Next were two boisterous buddies jostling to see who could first descend the few red-carpeted steps from the tiny sanctuary to the even-smaller foyer. Mike grabbed his pastor in a bear hug. "Pastor, your preaching and teaching are getting better. You must really be spending some time with the Lord."

Don merely smiled humbly and thought, "You have no idea."

After they put on their thick winter jackets, Mike playfully pushed Stan. "Now, go on. We have to leave the pastor alone. He probably has more work to do."

Don held up his hands. "Hey, there is always more to do, but I really enjoy spending time with you two."

Stan stared at the ground for a minute, as Mike exited before him. "Pastor, last week, I was a little out of line. Will you forgive me?"

Don gazed at him. "Stan, I've already forgiven you."

As Stan passed Don, he stuck one hand up in the air in a farewell motion and the other hand went subtly to his face, to make sure no tears could be seen.

The Revealer took an opportunity to teach Don: "You people are emotional creatures. Your present situations overwhelm you and your emotions explode. That's why you have to look at the hearts of people, because their behavior will confuse you."

"I thought I could know their hearts by their behavior," Don said with a quizzical look on his face.

"Most times, that's the case," the Revealer said, continuing His lesson. "But when people are overwhelmed or feel like they're spiraling out of control, their behavior can contradict or even be the opposite of what's in their hearts."

Don thought he understood. "So, if their behavior is negative because of stress or fear in their lives, I should not assume that's the substance of their hearts."

The Revealer zeroed in even more. "Don, have you ever overreacted about something minor and later thought, 'Why was I so worked up?'"

"Many times." Don said, counting his fingers.

"But your behavior wasn't exactly portraying your heart," said the Revealer.

"Yes. So, when someone acts out of the ordinary or their behavior is not consistent with what it has been, that may not be what's in their hearts," Don said.

Margaret stood close to Chloe as she bundled up Baby Emma. "Now, if you need any help the next couple of days, I'll be right there," Margaret offered.

Chloe sighed. "I might take you up on that."

The Revealer grabbed Don's shoulder as Margaret and Chloe continued to gather the diaper bag and the blanket and balance Baby Emma. "Remember last week, when you were so frustrated because Margaret was always chasing rabbits instead of staying on track?"

Don thought back, even though last week seemed a lifetime ago. "Yes, I was pretty frustrated."

The Revealer walked over to where the two were fussing over Baby Emma. He smiled directly at the baby and she started cooing. "Margaret, she just loves you so much!" Chloe squealed.

Don almost corrected her, but then came to his senses. With Baby Emma wrapped in more layers than an onion and of all her possessions secured, Margaret and Chloe gave Don a quick "See you on Sunday" as they ambled out the door.

"Will I ever completely learn how to know people's hearts?" Don asked.

The Revealer placed His hand on Don's shoulder. "We will talk about that in a few minutes. First, Debbie is coming up to see you before she goes to Dairy Queen."

Don had forgotten that Debbie was still at the church cleaning up. He started downstairs to help her but she met him on the middle step.

"Honey, I was just coming down to help you. Can I do anything?" Don asked.

"No, it's taken care of," she said, and nestled into the arms of her husband as they walked back to the small foyer.

Debbie started walking toward her coat dangling on the metal hanger, but suddenly stopped. "Don, can we go into the sanctuary for just a few minutes? We had such a good night tonight and I want to thank God for it."

The Revealer lifted His hand with His palm upward in a motion directing Don toward the sanctuary. Debbie was excited. "Erin's friend came and she really paid attention. I'm pleased that her mother brought her tonight."

Don and Debbie walked hand-in-hand and sat in the last pew.

It hit Don that he had not even asked about the mother picking up her daughter. "Honey, I'm sorry, but with all that went on up here, I didn't even ask about how it went when the mother picked up her daughter."

"It was wonderful," Debbie said, her face glowing. "We were able to talk for a few minutes as the kids cleaned up the crayons. She mentioned that when she was a little girl, she used to go to church with her grandmother, but when the grandmother passed away, the mother never went back. I sensed a sadness in her heart about that."

The Revealer stood near the back of the sanctuary, giving Don and Debbie space, but when Don looked back at him, the Revealer nodded His head in agreement with Debbie.

"I invited her to church on Sunday and I really hope they will come," Debbie said.

Don agreed. "I invited her, too, and I know your little evangelist daughter will be working on her daughter at school, too."

"She's just like her father," Debbie snickered.

"Honey, she is more like her mother and for that, I'm exceedingly grateful," Don teased.

"Don, I've been watching you this past week and something is different," Debbie said in a more serious tone.

"Is there anything wrong?" Don said with a hint of defensiveness.

"No, no," Debbie reassured him, "but you just seem like you have been in the presence of God more."

Don tilted his head to the side.

"In the presence of God, like I have been spending more time with Him?"

Debbie smiled and joy splashed across her face.

"Yes. Have you been? I mean, tell me, have you been doing anything different?"

Don was moved by her insistence. "God tells me to spend more time with you and the kids."

She rolled her green eyes. "Seriously . . ."

Don interrupted her, "Seriously! The . . . I mean, God has been telling me to spend more time with you and the kids." He almost said "the Revealer."

Debbie pondered that. "Yes, spending time together is important and it's been wonderful, but I just feel that you're growing spiritually."

"Yes, I am, but another lesson I'm learning is whenever I start to learn more about God, there's so much more. It seems when one question is answered that five more pop up."

"That's why we are going to spend eternity with God," Debbie chuckled. "We're going to learn more about Him forever and ever."

"Debbie, I want to thank you because you teach me so much about God," Don said, moving closer to his wife.

Debbie pulled her head away, not because she was rejecting him moving closer, but because she was shocked. "How do I teach you so much about God?"

"You have a pure heart. That's one of the first things I saw in you when we were in school, and that's one of the greatest reasons I love you," said Don.

"Don, I love you and I see God in your heart all the time, too." Debbie said.

Don was incredulous at how many ways he was blessed by the Father. As he held his wife, she asked him to say a prayer before she went to join the rowdy entourage of church people consuming ice cream at Dairy Queen.

Don nodded his head as he drew his wife even more tightly, but, at first, found himself speechless. He was basking in a flood of amazement. Just a week ago, he had been so frustrated after the Bible Study, he launched into a tirade against God. Now, he was inundated with how good God had been to him and his family.

After a couple of minutes, Don prayed, "Father, You have been better to me than I deserve. Please forgive me for the many times when I get wrapped up in myself. Forgive me for the times that my heart has been so crowded that I pushed You out. Father, thank You for my family. Other than being saved, my wife is the greatest gift I could have ever received. And Father, forgive me when I have taken her for granted. Father, thank You for the kids. Thank You for their hearts and let me have the childlike faith that they have. Father, thank You for the church, thank You for the Sorrellses coming to know You, and thank You for how much they love You. Father, I just can't say thank You enough."

At that point, words were unnecessary. Don opened his eyes and saw legions of winged spirit beings, angels, filling the sanctuary. They raised their hands in worship as they bowed down before the Revealer. The face of the Revealer glowed in a dazzling manner and Don wished that Debbie would have been able to see it.

After a few minutes of holy stillness, Debbie squeezed Don and said, "I have to go, honey, but I felt we were surrounded by the heavenly host."

Don shook his head in amazement and thought, "How does she know?"

The Revealer answered him. "She has a pure heart."

Don and Debbie kissed each other sweetly and Don pulled her into him for one last quick embrace before she left. She playfully pushed him away, admonishing him, "None of that, or else I won't go to Dairy Queen." They both laughed.

Debbie rose and started toward the foyer to get her coat. "Are you coming to Dairy Queen with me?"

"No, there are a few loose ends I have to tie up here. You go and have fun and I'll be home later," Don responded.

As she put on her jacket, she said, "Do you want me to bring anything home for you?"

Don stood and waved. "No, I have everything I could ever want."

Debbie turned and left and Don yelled out, "Be careful driving. I love you."

"I love you, too," Debbie replied.

"So, I'm a loose end now," needled the Revealer.

"Well, theologically, You and the Father and the Son are the beginning and the end, the alpha and omega," Don smugly suggested.

Don sat in the pew and the Revealer walked toward him with an intense look in his eyes. "Don, we don't have much more time together. Is there anything you would like to ask Me? I may or may not answer you, but you can ask."

Don had actually received two gifts last Wednesday evening after an exasperating Bible Study. The first was the ability to see people's hearts, but the second gift, which in many ways was far greater than the first, was to spend time with the Revealer. Now, that was coming to a close and Don's mind swirled.

"I haven't really thought about any questions to ask You. This last week went so fast!" Don found himself tongue-tied.

"Life goes so quickly," the Revealer agreed. "The Word talks about how the lives of people are like a vapor or a vanishing mist."

Don tried to collect his racing, divergent thoughts and tie them together, but all he could think about was whether he had learned enough this past week. Don, hesitant to ask because he was afraid of the response, said, "I do have a question for You. Did I learn as much as I should have? Did I do a good job with our time?"

The Revealer came around to the side of pew and stood next to Don. "Why are you asking these types of questions?"

Don seemed flabbergasted. "I don't know. . . . I guess I just don't want to think that I squandered this opportunity. I appreciate our time and have learned more than I believe I could have."

"Don, We know how much this last week has meant to you and We know that you have grown spiritually," the Revealer said.

Don managed to put the rapid hodgepodge running through his head together into coherent thoughts. "OK. Since I have grown, will I have an easier time resisting the enemy?"

The Revealer glanced toward the ground in a forlorn manner and then gazed piercingly into Don's eyes.

"No, because you have experienced this gift, the enemy is going to come after you harder and more often."

Don's face reflected the shock running through his soul.

"But You'll be there to help me when he comes after me, won't You?"

"I'm always with you and We will never leave you, but there will be times when you feel that you're walking through a valley of shadows all by yourself," the Revealer said. "Tomorrow, he's going to attack you in ways in which you've never been attacked before. He's going to challenge every lesson you've learned. He's going to go after every person in the church. Even during the ministers' meeting tomorrow, the enemy is going to show himself."

Don shifted his weight uncomfortably.

"But why? We had such a wonderful meeting last week. Why can't the enemy leave me alone?"

"Because you are stronger now than you were a week ago. But don't worry, I have already prompted Pastor Liddle to spend some time with you after the meeting, so he can encourage you."

More questions popped up in Don's mind.

"But what if he gets busy? But what if he doesn't listen to You? But what if I get a flat tire and can't even go to Bedford?"

Calmly, the Revealer responded, "Don, slow down. What's in your heart right now?"

"Fear!" Don exclaimed, in a panic.

"Exactly. I'm still right here with you and never, ever forget, Don, that I'll always be with you! You're going to be all right," the Revealer reassured him.

Don took a deep breath and started to focus. "Is there anything that I should have learned but I didn't this week?"

"That's a valid question, Don, but remember you are not going to know everything. You are in process," the Revealer gently said.

Thoughts, ideas and words were coming rapid-fire to Don's mind. He didn't seem to be able to collect them.

"But I have so much to ask You!"

The Revealer tilted his head down and grinned. "Oh, I'm still going to be talking to you and teaching you, and, every now and then, I'll even be chewing you out."

"How are we going to talk to each other?" Don seemed stunned.

"Every time you read the Bible; I'll be there pointing things out for you. Every time your conscience moves you to action or not to do something, it will be Me prodding you. Every time you see the sweetness in the hearts of your wife and children, you'll see My smiling face."

Don felt a comfort come over him. "And every time the enemy comes after me in the front seat of my car, You'll be sitting in the back seat with me."

"When the enemy starts talking, you kick him to the back seat and make sure I'm in the front seat next to you!" the Revealer said with a mock snarl.

"That's what I should have done the other day," Don said, attempting to suppress a chuckle.

"Could have, should have, would have. Don. We can rehash and relive yesterday, but the important matter is to choose to focus on the Father today, and that will take care of tomorrow. Let's continue our talk downstairs in your office."

Don walked to the wall and flipped off the light switch for the sanctuary. Before he descended the few steps to the tiny foyer, he looked back and remembered how the heavenly hosts, as Debbie had called them, had filled the room. Then he turned and headed toward his office.

When Don entered his office, the Revealer was standing behind his chair. "Here, come sit down."

Don did as instructed.

"Last week, when I met you, you had a rough time taking off your tie. You almost ripped your head off," the Revealer teased.

Don forgot that he was still wearing a tie because when services were over, one of the first things he usually did was to remove it from around his neck. Don laughed and gently pulled his tie away from his neck. "I guess things went a little differently this week."

"They did, but no matter how things go, you can always come and spend time with Us," the Revealer said.

Don nodded his head in agreement.

"I know that now. One of the hard things for us as people is that we can't see You or the Father or the Son, so we forget that You're always here."

The Revealer raised a finger and started pointing around the office.

"Don, you may not see a physical embodiment of us, but look around your office. When you see a Bible, you can hear the words spoken to you by the Father. When you look at the clock and see the passage of time, you can know that We always were and always will be. When you look at the picture Nathaniel drew for you one day during service, you can see how much love the Father has for you, his son."

Don attempted to demonstrate his understanding.

"The Son said, 'Let him who has eyes see and he who has ears hear.'"

The Revealer slowly nodded his head in agreement.

"Don, come stand over here with Me." The Revealer directed him to stand in front of his door, which had a full-length mirror attached to it.

"What do you see?" asked the Revealer.

"A happy man, still wearing a tie," Don smiled. "And I can see You, right behind me."

Slowly, the Revealer walked him through this.

"Don, soon you will not be able to visually see Me in this form, but never forget I'm right here with you."

A peace passed over Don like none he had ever experienced. He was transfixed with tranquility and his heart felt fuller than ever before. The Revealer reached up and placed both hands on Don's shoulders in an act of affirmation.

Then, the room shook, but nothing moved. Don underwent a sensation of being dizzy but stood still and straight. The lighting of the room became intensely vivid. It was brighter, not because more lights had been turned on, but because the presence of the Lord was near.

Don remembered some of these feelings from last week, but now it was different. Last week, he was almost repelled because of fear and naivete, but this week, he longed to be in the presence of the Father. Don knew that he stood on holy ground.

A booming voice spoke, reverberating through every corridor of Don's heart. "My son, last week you asked for the gift of seeing the hearts of people. Did you receive that?"

It was not a question, but the Father prodding Don's soul.

"Yes, Father. Thank you for that beautiful gift. I learned a lot, but there's so much more I need to learn."

"Yes, there is, my son. I'm happy that you learned many lessons and you're right, you will be learning more and more," the Father instructed.

Don was in awe. He knew he was in the presence of the Living Lord, the God who created the universe just by the intonation of His voice, the God who said, "Let there be light" and the skies erupted with illumination, eliminating the darkness. Don heard from the Deity who, when He was here in the form of the Son, had told a dead Lazarus to come forth from a tomb and a living Lazarus walked out of the grave.

Don's mind seemed to process all of these thoughts at one time, but he also was more complete than ever before. Don didn't want to appear brazen.

"Father, why have You been so good to me?"

"You are my son. You are my special creation. I knew when I formed you in the womb of your mother that one day, I would be speaking to you in your office."

The voice of the Father commanded an authority to be respected but also trusted at the same time.

"Donald, I have entrusted much to you. You are a husband. Love your wife with all your heart. Treat her as the treasure she is. You are a father. Love your children and teach them how I take care of you and how I love them. You are a pastor, a high calling because when you stand to talk about Me, you are transcending from the ordinary into the extraordinary. You are a man of God. The enemy is going to come after you, but I don't ever want you to forget that you are more than a conqueror through My Son. When He vanquished the enemy at Calvary, the Son gave you the same power. When you are struggling, remember the time you spent with the Revealer. When the Son returned to Me, He sent the Revealer to be with people. Just as He taught you, spoke to you, was patient with you, He will continue to do so."

With each word, love flowed from the Father, covering Don as if warming, healing oil was slowly being poured over his head.

Don raised his hands, palms up, in worship, and received the love of the Father. Tears of joy, contentment, and gladness streamed slowly down his face. He felt the firm embrace of the Revealer's hands on his shoulders. Don didn't want this to end. He wanted to stay surrounded by the majesty of the Father forever.

"Donald, I do have one last question for you," the Father said.

Don's eyes sprang open as he stuttered. "Yes, Lord, anything."

"How is your heart?"

The question at first seemed to be basic, but Don knew its depth could not be comprehended.

One of the first thoughts that flew through Don's mind was the chorus of a well-known hymn, "It is well with my soul."

"Guard your heart. If anything impure attacks you, let Us cleanse your heart. Fill your heart with Us." The kind words flowed from the Father's heart to Don.

The room reverted to normal, even though nothing had actually changed, but everything had. Don looked in the mirror at the Revealer.

"The Father asked me about my heart."

"Yes." the Revealer said, returning Don's gaze.

"This whole week has not been about me knowing the hearts of others, but me learning about my own heart," Don said, as if a light suddenly had been switched on.

"Yes," the Revealer said.

"Because when I am working on my heart, making sure that I'm where I should be with You and the Father and the Son, everything else will fall into place."

Don's heart was elated.

"Yes," the Revealer agreed.

"That's it!" Don continued in an excited voice. "You were sent to me to reveal my heart. You were here this week so I would learn to keep my heart pure, so that I could help the hearts of others."

"Yes," the Revealer smiled.

"Wow, I don't know what to say."

"You don't have to say anything," the Revealer gently told Don. "Let your heart talk and when it does, people will see Us."

"My heart and I thank you for this past week," Don said, aware that it might sound trite.

The Revealer firmly squeezed Don's shoulders.

"In just a moment, you will not see Me in this form, but remember, I'm always speaking to you."

Don reached back over his left shoulder with his right hand, placing it on top of the Revealer's hand. "I am going to miss seeing You in this form."

"I know. But never forget, I'm always with you."

Don moved his hand from his shoulder and watched as the Revealer slowly faded from sight. It was not sudden, but as gradual as the light of the morning gently piercing the darkness. Don noticed that, as the face of

Revealer vanished, it contained a huge smile and His eyes vibrantly shone with love.

Don didn't want to move. He stood motionless in front of the mirror, staring at his reflection. It was then he heard a familiar voice ringing in his head settling in his heart.

"Remember, I am always with you."